A PREARRANGED LOVE

ANUSHA VISHNAMPET

JAICO PUBLISHING HOUSE

Ahmedabad Bangalore Bhopal Bhubaneswar Chennai
Delhi Hyderabad Kolkata Lucknow Mumbai

Published by Jaico Publishing House
A-2 Jash Chambers, 7-A Sir Phirozshah Mehta Road
Fort, Mumbai - 400 001
jaicopub@jaicobooks.com
www.jaicobooks.com

© Anusha Vishnampet

A PREARRANGED LOVE
ISBN 978-81-8495-398-5

First Jaico Impression: 2013

No part of this book may be reproduced or utilized in
any form or by any means, electronic or
mechanical including photocopying, recording or by any
information storage and retrieval system,
without permission in writing from the publishers.

Page design and layouts: Special Effects, Mumbai

Printed by

*To anyone who has ever wanted to
do something memorable in life.*

If I can do it, you can too — so get on with it!

Chapter One

"Why don't you try meeting him? He might turn out to be the man of your dreams..." said Rekha's mother Sheela, with all the persuasive skills of a used car salesman.

Rekha burst out laughing. She said, "Mom, the man of my dreams is determined to remain a bachelor and spend all his time in Italy." After a dramatic pause, she said, "I am talking about George Clooney."

Sheela was a dauntless mother who doted on her daughter. Her only wish was to see her daughter happily married. But she also understood Rekha's quirky, curious nature. She vividly remembered Rekha's childhood; when most kids were wondering where babies came from and asked their parents about it, Rekha had taken a different approach. One day after school, Rekha's

A Prearranged Love

teacher said sheepishly, "your daughter asked me how babies are born and I wasn't sure what to tell her." When Sheela asked Rekha why she had gone to her Science teacher, Rekha had explained reasonably, "She knows about fish babies, hen babies and cow babies so I thought she'd know about real babies too."

Sheela pulled herself out of those sweet memories and tried once more. "Listen, you don't have to commit yourself for life. Just meet Arjun once, talk to him and maybe you'll like him."

Rekha smiled and said, "That I am willing to do; I have to admit I am curious to go on a date arranged by my mother. How cool are we!" she said mockingly.

"Great, I'll give you his phone number and you can set up a place and time. And don't forget – don't be out too late; some men only need an inch to take a mile!" Sheela was a mother, all said and done.

"Not so cool, after all," Rekha added.

"I am cool, not stupid." Sheela wagged her index finger.

Rekha looked at herself in the mirror and was pleased with her appearance. She looked quite nice, if she did say so herself. She had debated mentally for some time on what to wear for a blind-date arranged by her mother, for a no-strings-attached-but-could-potentially-end-up-in-marriage meeting. She settled for a red, green and brown tie-dye skirt with a red embroidered top. There – colourful and casual.

Once Sheela had given Arjun's phone number to her, Rekha had not seen any point in putting off the meeting and decided she might as well have some fun along the way. So she had called Arjun and explained that she had gotten his details from her mother who knew his mother and she would like to meet him for coffee; but she didn't want him to think she was some love-crazed loser stalking him.

Whoa! She had actually asked a guy out on a date. More power to women!

"Are you sure you should be wearing a skirt? It makes you look even shorter." Sheela asked worriedly.

"Mom, I think he'll know how short I am when he sees me. Short of wearing stilts, there is no fooling anyone!" Rekha said with exasperation. She was short, not stunted. After all, five foot two inches was a perfectly normal height for an Indian woman, especially since she was small-framed.

"Fine, fine, get going otherwise you will be late!" urged Sheela, resigned to her daughter's petite physique. And anyway, it was too late to worry about the lack of a height gene in the family. Sheela herself was about Rekha's height and her late husband, Ramkumar had been of average height.

Rekha arrived at the Deli-Hiway, a stylish coffee shop in one of the newly-opened malls in Hyderabad. Arjun and she had arranged to meet at five thirty at the cafe and it was almost time. She spotted an empty table in a quiet corner and trotted over to a cushy chair and sat on it. She was idly perusing the menu, the Schnookie Brookie orange drink sounded interesting; maybe she would order that.

As she gazed around, she noticed a tall man dressed in grey trousers and a pale blue shirt entering the cafe. She normally would not have paid attention but since

A Prearranged Love

she was waiting for the 'man of her dreams', her *guy'dar* was well-tuned.

She stood up and waved to catch his attention and he looked her way, a little surprised and then walked towards her table. Up close, Rekha decided he looked cute and thought maybe this date was not such a bad idea after all. He was very tall, and appeared to be lean yet fit. His eyes were bright and clear, accompanied by a straight nose and square jaw. He must have said something but she had missed it because she was busy staring at him! 'Earth to, Rekha!' She mentally chided herself.

"Sorry, I am Rekha and you must be Arjun," she said and extended her hand, then wondered if that was too business-like for a date. Never mind, she was not about to go around hugging strange men, no matter how cute they were.

"Hi, nice to meet you." Arjun replied as they shook hands. He had a nice grip, warm and dry and his hand closed around her much smaller one, enveloping it nicely. It was a good sign that he did not have clammy palms.

Handshake over, they both sat down and Rekha decided to start the conversational ball rolling.

"Would you like to order now or talk for a while?"

"Umm, sure why don't we order something first?" Arjun suggested. He looked around for a waiter.

Only then did Rekha realise that Arjun had not smiled at all since they met. Not even the polite, insincere one that people give in strange situations, nor had he looked at her, except briefly. Her instinct was telling her that something was wrong and she did not want to sit through an uncomfortable coffee to find out the reason.

"Are you okay? You look worried. I hope this is not an inconvenient time to meet." Maybe he was preoccupied with some work-related issues.

"Umm, yeah it's fine." Again, Rekha noticed he did not smile or say more.

Okay, this wasn't going well. Rekha decided to give it one more shot. "Mom said you work as a software developer. Do you enjoy your work?"

"Yeah, its fine." He looked around impatiently.

Rekha decided to be blunt. "Listen, I know it's strange to be set up on a blind date by our mothers and I understand if you feel uncomfortable doing this."

Hearing that, Arjun seemed to relax a little. He said, "I'm so relieved that you feel awkward too. I wasn't sure how to go about telling you."

"Telling me what?" Rekha thought he was going to confess he had a girlfriend or some such thing. She knew it! All the good ones are always taken!

"Well, you are not what I expected. I mean, I thought you would be taller..." Arjun seemed to realise what he was saying, and then quickly backtracked, "I mean, my mom said you were of medium height."

Rekha could not believe what she was hearing. And she had a feeling it was only going to get worse. Controlling her irritation, she asked with forced politeness, "Yes, I am shorter than the average woman, but why does that make you uncomfortable?"

"It doesn't make me uncomfortable. I was surprised because I was imagining somebody taller and with longer hair. Not that your hair is bad or anything."

"I know my hair is not bad. In fact it's interesting and different." It was curly, wild and just reached her shoulders; she had grown past the angst-ridden teenage years when she had cursed her hair for being so unusual.

"It certainly is different." He said with what looked like a smirk. It seemed he was determined to be a jerk and Rekha could not believe that the date was going so horrendously wrong. Sure, she had expected it to be awkward at first but had assumed it would get better once the ice was broken. At worst, she had expected to be bored but not even in her most pessimistic musings had she thought that she would be stuck with a shallow, rude and sexist man. It was obvious from his words that he thought all women should have the traditional allure of long hair and a tall, lithe physique.

"Let me see if I've got it right. Your mother set you up with me, hoping we would talk and get to know each other and then, maybe decide to get married. But to you, hair and body obviously make a stronger marriage!" She could not quite contain her indignation.

"Come on, don't take it personally, it was just an observation." He held up his hands in defence.

"Oh, I am not taking it personally; I am taking it as an offence against all women that men like you think you can objectify women and ignore any shred of character or personality completely." Rekha countered angrily.

"Oh, you are one of those feminists, eh?"

"Yes, I am a feminist. To be anything else in this day and age is just being ignorant. I can't believe our mothers thought you and I would make a good match. What were they thinking?"

"Hey, there is no need to insult me just because I said that you are not my type."

"Oh, don't take it personally. It was just an observation." She got tremendous satisfaction in parroting his words to him.

"Touché." He smiled an easier smile this time. He seemed to be more relaxed now. "Honestly, it's nothing personal, Rekha. I've had a few girlfriends in the past and they were all tall and I do like long hair on a woman."

Now he was explaining his 'type' to her! It was too much for her to take in. "Really? Why didn't you marry your previous girlfriends?"

"Well, I wasn't really ready for marriage and so the relationships came to a gradual end." He shrugged, as if he had proved his point. "Don't tell me women don't dream of tall, dark and handsome men."

"Well, I am telling you we don't. That was a myth perpetuated by men like you to justify their questionable tastes."

"Are you telling me that women don't like good-looking guys? C'mon, I saw you ogling when I entered." His point made, he sat back smugly.

"And did you see my disgust about two minutes later? 'Cause, that's when you started talking."

"Hey!" he pretended to look offended.

"It's true! You were cute till you opened your mouth and started enlightening me about my 'hair' and 'height' take it from me – there is nothing sadder than a cute but sexist pig. So much potential gone to waste." she tsked-tsked mockingly.

He laughed, a delighted, full-throated laugh and despite herself, Rekha started to smile. Dammit! She had never been able to resist laughter. When people around her laughed, she found it infectious, as if they were inviting her to join in. His was particularly magnetic and changed his face from cute to heart-stopping.

He looked startled to see her smile, probably because she had been so indignant just a few minutes ago and the transition took him by surprise.

There was an awkward pause once the laughter stopped and she looked at her watch, just to have something to do. Goodness, she had not realised it but their sparring had taken almost twenty minutes.

"Well, I don't think this discussion is going anywhere. You don't think I am your type and I especially don't want to be your type." She stood up and said "It's been interesting meeting you." She raised her eyebrows at 'interesting' hoping he understood her sarcasm.

"Oh, so soon? We were just beginning to have fun. What should I tell my Mom?" he asked sardonically.

"Well, why don't you tell her the truth? It should be fun for her to know her son's choices better." Any self-respecting woman would be appalled knowing his criteria for an 'ideal woman'.

"For such a shorty, you don't pull any punches, do you?" he asked amusedly.

"Maybe it's time to buy you a drink. Would you like it on your lap or over your head?" she snapped.

He laughed his infectious laugh again. "This has been an unexpected evening, in many ways. Thank you for that, at least."

She glared at him and turned towards the door. Thank god, that was over. Now she had to report back to her mother. Maybe this would put the brakes on Sheela's matchmaking schemes, because after meeting McJerky, she was wondering if all men had the same idea when they were looking for a wife. If so, she would rather stay single the rest of her life than get hitched to any of those princes.

❧

Arjun watched with a smile as Rekha strode away from the café. What a feisty little thing she was. She had really surprised him.

Arjun was surprised at himself too. He normally was not so outspoken, especially not to women he had just met. He had only agreed to meet her because his mother had pestered him about settling down. Then Rekha had called him to ask if they could meet up. He couldn't say no and by then, he had just wanted to get it over with.

He had arrived at the restaurant and seen a stylish, stunning girl seated alone. He had been tempted by the possibility that she was Rekha but that notion had proven incorrect when that hottie had been joined by a female friend. Then he had seen Rekha, all five-feet-two-inches with that wild mane of hair and those curious eyes. He had been caught off-guard because he had always pictured himself with a tall woman, hell, he was taller than the average guy and he found it more convenient if he didn't have to stoop down to kiss a woman. That could break a guy's back!

Of course, he probably had not explained himself very well to Rekha. But rather than get hurt or, even worse, start making a scene, she had actually questioned his intelligence and taste. She had even sensed his unease right away and asked him directly about it. That was one sharp lady.

And he was not as shallow as she thought him to be. Once he had relaxed a little, he had noticed that she was quite cute – petite, in spite of her curly hair and all. Then she had gone and smiled at him momentarily forgetting the argument and revealed the most adorable dimples he had ever seen; not just one on each cheek but also tiny dent-like ones at the corners of her mouth. The image

A Prearranged Love

still lingered in his mind. Her face was tailor-made for a black and white photograph — her expressions would more than make up for the lack of colour.

Not that he was planning to photograph her. She was certainly interesting but he was not even sure if he wanted to get married now and as he had told her, she was not his type. If he decided to get married, it would be to a pretty, easy-going woman who would adapt to his habits and quirks, not a feisty, outspoken feminazi regardless of how cute her dimples were.

Rekha prepared herself mentally as she drove her tangerine coloured scooty into the driveway and parked it under a tree. She didn't want her faithful scooter, Tanya, to get hot. With her shiny and vivid appearance, she was hot enough already.

She was just delaying the inevitable, she knew. Taking a deep breath, she walked up the short staircase and unlocked the front door, made of solid wood with little artsy motifs carved on it. Normally, just entering her home, with its wooden and colourful interiors relaxed her, but today was not one of those days.

"Rekha, are you back already?" Sheela rose from the sofa where she was seated, piles of papers on the table in front of her, and a pen poised in her hand. Rekha had forgotten that it was term break, which meant Sheela was marking English papers for college students whose interest in the characterisation of Elizabeth Bennett and Eliza Doolittle was almost non-existent. Rekha occasionally gave her a hand, as she loved reading and found the whole exercise quite amusing. Today, however,

Sheela was not going to be distracted.

"So, what happened? Did you talk and get to know each other? What did he say?" Sheela was clearly ready to play 'twenty questions' and Rekha was irritated just thinking about the answers. This is what she got for going along with her mother's matchmaking plans!

"Oh, it went extremely well... I am in fact coming back from the Marriage Registrar's office! Arjun and I liked each other so much that we decided we just couldn't wait to make it official!" She said sarcastically.

"Didn't you like him?"

"Ah, the problem wasn't with *me*. Apparently, I am not tall enough to be a suitable bride for Mr. Arjun Kalyan! And he is not a fan of my curly hair, either."

"What? He said that to you?" Thank heavens; Sheela was as appalled as Rekha had been. It soothed her offended sensibilities.

"Yup, about two minutes after we met, he said I wasn't his type because his previous girlfriends were tall and had long hair and by the way, he asked me not to take it personally."

"How could you not take that personally? Men!" Sheela sighed and said with the resignation of somebody who had been through similar trials herself.

"Mom, to add to it he called me a hypocritical feminist."

"Really?" Now Sheela looked amused. "I bet you took that really well."

Despite herself Rekha smiled and said "You win! I called him a sexist pig and told him I hope his mother knows what a lovely son she has."

"That was harsh, even for you. You have to know though, Sunita is nothing like her son; she is a lovely

A Prearranged Love

person. It'll probably disappoint her that this match won't be going anywhere. It is not going anywhere, right?" Sheela wanted confirmation.

"Mom, I would be crazy to even contemplate a life with him after this. Imagine actually being married to him... I would have to change myself from head-to-toe just to please him." Rekha shuddered at the thought.

"I understand, but I am disappointed. I was hoping something would come out of your meeting." Sheela sighed again and was about to go back to her exam papers when she remembered something and a mischievous twinkle came into her eyes.

"I almost forgot; how is he to look at?" Sheela asked curiously. "I know it doesn't matter but at least tell me he is balding and paunchy so I'll feel better."

Rekha groaned and then laughed. "I am so going to disappoint you. He was tall, cute and had the most infectious laugh I have ever heard. It was so nice that I almost joined him when he was laughing at me!"

"Too bad, life is just not fair." Sheela said. "Now, do you want to help me go through these papers or do I have to read alone on how Alicia Silverstone portrayed a better Emma than Jane Austen?"

Rekha's mood instantly lifted, "Ooh, gimme!"

"I hope I am not disturbing you." Sunita, Arjun's mother said apologetically to Sheela. She was of medium height, with a round and kind face, dressed in a pale green cotton sari. Sheela was surprised and a little wary because she had a feeling this was no casual visit. Recalling how eager she had been to hear about Rekha's date yesterday, she could understand how Sunita must be feeling.

"No need to apologise, Sunita. My college is closed for the holidays now so you really didn't interrupt anything."Sheela ushered her into the living room and towards the sofa.

"Would you like something to drink? Tea, coffee or water..."

"I would love a glass of water, thank you."

Sheela fetched the water for Sunita, gave it to her and sat down.

"So let me guess, are you here to talk about our dubious future as matchmakers?" Sheela asked wryly.

Sunita laughed and said, "I am glad you said that because I came to find out what happened yesterday. Arjun was very close-mouthed about the whole thing and when I pressed him for answers, all I got was, "I don't think Rekha and I are suitable for each other."

"I can give you some more details but I think he gave you the gist of it." Sheela quickly explained Arjun's reaction on meeting Rekha and Rekha's own reaction. She knew Sunita through mutual friends and she liked and enjoyed her company. She did not want to lose her friendship because of this little incident.

Sunita looked upset after hearing the story. She said, "I can't believe he was so rude to your daughter. I am so sorry, Sheela. He is generally well-mannered. I can't understand what got into him yesterday. It's one thing to not like somebody, but the things he said to her are not nice and I am glad Rekha gave him a piece of her mind."

"It's okay Sunita. Rekha is no timid school girl. I am sure she said some rude things too." 'Sexist pig' would definitely constitute rude, Sheela thought. "Listen, we gave it a shot and it didn't work out. I think they are both opinionated so it's probably a good thing that it ended without casualties," Sheela said with a smile.

"True, but it would have been lovely if they had hit it off....oh well, I guess it was not meant to be," Sunita said wistfully.

⌒∽⌒

Rekha parked her scooty, in the hot, glaring sun outside her office. She was running late and did not have the time to search for a shady spot so Tanya would just have to deal with it.

Holding her helmet in one hand and pushing open the glass doors to her office, Rekha stepped into the cool comfort of air-conditioning. A discreet and stylish sign in navy blue and orange said 'Flash Advertising & Marketing Solutions.' Rekha loved the office, with its navy blue decor with splashes of orange and lime green. No wonder she was drawn to a career in the visual media – colours had a profound impact on her, sometimes exciting, sometimes soothing but never indifferent.

Waving to Thomas, the receptionist, she walked into the main office and placed her helmet and bag on her desk. Suresh, her colleague and a client service executive on her team, greeted her with a smile and said, "Good, you are here. Boss got in early this morning and wants to have a meeting as soon as possible with you, Aditya Sammy and myself." Aditya was the team's account manager and Sammy (a.k.a Samanth), the designer.

"Boss" was Naveen Sharma, a smooth-talking, business-school educated entrepreneur who had started Flash seven years ago, after deciding he was his own boss and would not work for anybody else. He was highly ambitious but also a supportive and generous boss. At times, his practiced salesman-of-the-year facade irritated Rekha but it kept business thriving since somebody had to do it.

"Did he say what he wanted to talk about?" Rekha asked. It had to be something big, if he had to speak to the whole team together.

"No, but from the little-boy-on-his-birthday gleam in his eye, I would say it's new business for Flash." This came from Aditya who was dressed for success like a typical account manager in a suit, tie and that all-important leather folder.

"Great, that's fantastic! So what are we waiting for? Let's go find out what the news is."

"Sammy is not yet here," Suresh said.

Rekha rolled her eyes. Sometimes Sammy took the artistic-eccentric-designer routine too far. He was almost always late, wore ill-fitting clothes and tied his long hair in a ponytail. She knew it was deliberate, because he had once told her that a career in advertising was like being an actor; it was not enough to have the talent, you also had to look the part and cultivate the image. What irked her even more was that he was right. Rekha had seen the awe in their clients' eyes when they were introduced to him. Apparently artistic genius found expression through bad clothes and unkempt hair.

Almost as if her thoughts had conjured him up, Sammy ambled into the cubicle. Today, his usual attire of faded, tie-dyed tunic and faded jeans had an additional accessory; a black bandanna that he had fashioned like a head band.

"Good, you're here; boss wants to meet with us, so let's get moving." said Aditya. He was focused on the big picture and today that meant a potential cash flow. The rest were just pesky details.

Naveen looked up eagerly when they walked into his office. He was of average height and with a slightly bulky build and a receding hairline but carried himself energetically and always dressed like he was about to go on camera.

Gesturing them to sit, he looked at them and gave a broad smile. "Team, we have landed a new client, it's Softech, an IT company and they want to get a corporate video and TV, and print advertisements done by us." He looked expectantly at them.

"We knew it! That's great news, Naveen." Aditya was clearly very excited.

"Yeah, how did this happen? Tell us!" Rekha wanted to know the details.

Sammy said, "IT company? Those are nerds, Naveen. Does this mean I have to start dressing formally around here?"

They all laughed at that. Answering her question, Naveen said "I happened to meet the marketing head of Softech at a conference two weeks ago; we had studied at IIM together and we were reminiscing about those days. I later invited him to dinner, schmoozed him and there you have it." Naveen looked proudly at them.

"Your smooth-talking B-schooler connections do come in handy." Rekha said dryly.

"So when do we start working and how much are they paying us?" Suresh asked eagerly.

Naveen named a sum that was quite impressive and added, "but the contract hasn't yet been finalised and should be done in a couple of weeks. We need to impress them and get the deal signed, so we should start working soon. Rekha, you and Aditya need to meet with the Softech guys and begin work."

"Are you sure this deal will go through? Making a video is going to be expensive." Aditya asked with a little reservation.

"Don't worry; we won't start producing anything 'til the contract is signed. You guys can put together the brief, brainstorm and develop the concepts in the meanwhile." He hesitated and continued, "This doesn't leave this room, alright? The reason they need some intense marketing and promotion is because Softech is considering going public and raising capital early next year. So I am fairly confident about this one."

"In that case, we have no issues with meeting the Softech team. After all, they are going to be funding my new car." Aditya said jokingly.

Aditya and Rekha were very impressed by their new client's swanky headquarters. It was newly constructed, in Hyderabad's Technology Park and showcased a cylindrical multi-storeyed chrome and glass structure, painted a natural looking brick-red colour.

"Wow, this looks pretty posh. I hope the Softech guys are as nice as their building is..." Rekha said as she and Aditya drove into the visitors' parking lot. Aditya had decided to take his car as her Scooty wasn't 'impressive' enough for a new client and Rekha had not wanted to make the long commute to and from the city centre on a two-wheeler in the hot sun. Sometimes, being pretentious had its own perks!

"It doesn't matter if they are nice or not, Rekha.

Remember, it's not a sure thing yet and we have to do our best to convince them that Flash is their only option as we have the smarts, the strategy and the resources to do a good job for them. And we are affordable too, of course." Aditya was earnestly trying out his sales pitch on her.

"Hey, you don't have to convince me. All I want is to have a good meeting, with intelligent and focused people from Softech. The clearer their brief, the better I can put together a presentation for them with our ideas, budget and media plan." Rekha emphasised 'intelligent' because she had come across some strange requests from clients on occasion. Once, a client in the hospitality industry had come to her with an urgent request for advertising one of the restaurants in his hotel. When she had asked him what the pitch for the advertisement was, he had said, "Oh, we want to promote our Christmas buffet." There was nothing wrong with that except for the fact that it was July!

After registering at the reception, they were asked to wait for Sachin Kumar, the marketing manager who was one of their main contacts at Softech. Sachin arrived shortly, a trim, bespectacled, man with a friendly smile. Ushering them into the elevator, he said, "Let me introduce you to my marketing and product development teams. We have put together a presentation on the Softech vision, mission, products and services. Once you see that, you'll get a better idea of what we are looking for."

So far, so good, Rekha thought. At least everyone was clear on what they wanted to get out of this meeting.

Sachin led them to a conference room where she could already see some people seated around a boardroom table. Out of the corner of her eye, she saw somebody stand up and she instinctively turned to look.

Oh no, this couldn't be happening! That could not be Arjun Kalyan standing there with a smile on his face. She blinked and yes, it was him alright. So much for her prophetic request for intelligent clients.

Chapter Two

So many thoughts swirled around in Rekha's mind. Both the questions and the answers were supplied by her brain.

What the hell was he doing here? Arjun was a software developer, remember?

Did she have to be nice to him? Considering that he was part of the company and clearly part of the briefing team, yes, it would be a good idea to be nice to him.

Had she really called him a sexist pig? Yes and that had not been such a good idea...

Meanwhile, Sachin was introducing her and Aditya to everyone else seated and the lone standing man too. Then it was time to sit back and understand Softech. Rekha forced herself to concentrate on the PowerPoint presentation. This was her chance to demonstrate

Flash's worth to the team around the table and not waste it rehashing the disastrous date three days ago.

Thankfully, the presentation was both interesting and brief, so her mental discipline was not tested much while she took notes. Softech was a small but fast-growing software company and it developed and sold software products for the manufacturing and aviation sector. Rekha had dealt with clients in the entertainment, beauty and hospitality industries before and this was going to be very new and technical, but she had always been a quick learner so she was looking forward to the assignment. Sachin then took over the discussion and gave some information on their marketing requirements and expectations.

She looked around the table and unwittingly caught Arjun's eye. He raised one eyebrow and smiled knowingly. So he was enjoying this, thought Rekha. Reminding herself to be civil, she politely smiled back at him. Apparently she had not been very convincing, because his smile just got bigger.

Then it was their turn to introduce Flash. Aditya ran through the slides with practiced ease and Rekha filled in the gaps. When it was over, Sachin switched off the projector and said "Sorry I have to rush as I have another meeting. I'll get someone to show you around the building and maybe briefly introduce you guys to the General Manager."

He then gestured to Arjun, who looked only too willing to be of help. "Aditya, Rekha meet Arjun, he is the team leader for one of our Development divisions and will take you around." Looking at Arjun, he said "Check with GM's PA if he has a minute for introductions, okay?"

"Don't worry Sachin; I will take good care of them." Arjun said. Was that her paranoid mind working or did that sound just a little bit evil, Rekha wondered.

"Alright guys, it was great meeting you. We will be in touch then. Bye!" Rekha and Aditya chorused byes as Sachin left the room.

❧

"So, shall we begin guys?" Arjun asked like a well-trained tourist guide.

"Sure, thanks for showing us around." Aditya said graciously.

"Oh, it's my pleasure." He looked at her when he said that, so she knew she had not been paranoid earlier.

"So, tell me, you must be meeting a lot of interesting people in your profession, being in advertising and all." He said conversationally as he showed them around the open-plan office and cafeteria. The beautifully landscaped lawns and gardens were visible from the hallway.

"Oh yeah, we get some weird characters occasionally. Thankfully all our clients are really great and easy to work with." Aditya piped in; he was wary of 'word of mouth' advertising so he always spoke of clients in a good light, no matter how nutty they were.

"So Rekha, you are the copywriter and concept person. You must have some good stories." OK, he really was pushing it. If someone else had said the same thing to her, she would have just thought they were very interested in her work but she knew better with him.

"Oh, they are not very interesting. Just regular work pressures and coming up with the best for our clients." Oh god, she cringed mentally. Now she sounded like Aditya.

"Oh well, I am sure you'll find things here very interesting."

Just then Aditya spotted someone across the cubicles and waved to him.

"Can you excuse me for a minute? That's one of my friends over there. I'll say a quick hello and be back." Aditya strode across the office.

"So, the best for your clients, eh?" Arjun looked at her consideringly. "You realise this means you have to be very nice to me? No name-calling, no threats of physical violence and no insults. How will you ever survive?" he asked mockingly.

Goaded and with Aditya out of hearing distance, Rekha responded, "Well, I survived the date with you and today's meeting so I think I am quite under control. Don't worry, if I can't resist the temptation, I will be cursing you in my mind. So the next time you see me smile, you know what I am doing."

Arjun chuckled at that. "Thank god! I was wondering if it was the same Rekha I met days ago. But now I see that you are back in form."

"And don't you forget that!" Rekha retorted, determined to have the last word.

"So the Softech guys seemed like good clients." Rekha said to Aditya on their way back to the city.

"Yes, but I won't be happy till we have the contract signed and sealed. You never know with these things." Aditya pondered.

"Let's do our best to give them a good marketing plan and the rest is out of our control." Rekha said philosophically.

"Yes," agreed Aditya eagerly. "Let's have a brain-storming session back in office and start right away." Aditya continued, "By the way, Arjun is a good contact to have at Softech. He is from the Development team so he would be very knowledgeable about the business, products etc. Start developing a relationship with him and understanding the business. He could be very useful."

Rekha barely reigned in the impulse to roll her eyes. Developing a relationship with Arjun? Ha! Like that could happen! Then she wondered at her reaction. She had come across jerks before, both men and women. One did not work for six years without meeting all sorts of people. She had always tolerated them because she had to and she could not change people's attitudes. It helped that she didn't have to deal with them outside of work. Was she taking this thing with Arjun so seriously because he had rejected her? Maybe her pride was hurt and she didn't want to have anything to do with him again. If that was the case, then she just had to grow up and deal with it. Wasting a good opportunity at her work because a guy thought she was not his type was just silliness and she did not want to be vain and stupid.

Whether she was able to have a professional relationship with Arjun or not, she definitely had a good story to tell her mother.

That was hilarious, thought Arjun after seeing his visitors off. Life was so unpredictable. He had been bracing himself for another boring 'death by PowerPoint' meeting and then guess who walks in looking as surprised as he had been! He had almost forgotten about Rekha since their meeting. Clearly the lady had not forgotten anything.

Arjun had been very curious to see how she would react. He had half-expected her to walk off in a huff because she had certainly been indignant when they had parted ways the other day. But once again she had surprised him; she had ignored him for the most part, even when he had tried to provoke her. That was not very nice of him but when she had smiled that polite, indifferent smile at him during the presentation, a wicked impulse had gotten into him to see if he could get her riled up again.

She had looked so professional in her gray slacks and purplish shirt–oh yeah, women called that shade mauve. Count on them to come up with such froofy names for colours. Anyway, he had cheered up when she had retorted to his taunt about being nice. Maybe he was a masochist, but he felt energised by her quick comebacks and the prospect of the next round in their war of words.

He was impressed by how she held her own, even when she was amidst a bunch of techies who probably thought she was some intern fresh out of college or something. It was because she was so small. He had even heard one of his colleagues whisper to him during the meeting, to ask if Flash was in the habit of sending greenhorns to client meetings. That guy had shut up once she started her presentation.

Work was going to be very interesting for the next few months around here, Arjun thought to himself, strangely satisfied.

ॐ

A Prearranged Love

"You will never guess who I met today at one of our client's office!" Rekha exclaimed when she and Sheela were dining that evening. She loved these times with her mother. They often made dinner and ate together. Rekha's father Ramkumar had passed away in an accident when she was seven and since then it had been just the two of them. Though Rekha missed her father, his passing had brought her closer to Sheela and she cherished the relationship they both had. Most of her friends said she was really lucky to have a mother who was so modern and 'cool'. Rekha thought she was not only an amazing mother but also an awesome person. Not that they did not have disagreements or screaming matches but they never lasted long and were forgotten quickly.

"Who was it?" Sheela asked indulgently. Sheela was as involved in her daughter's work as Rekha was in Sheela's. She loved hearing about Rekha's day, the interesting people she met and discussing her ideas for work.

"Arjun Kalyan!" Rekha waited with anticipation to see Sheela's reaction and she wasn't disappointed. Sheela's eyes went wide and she stopped in mid-chew. Then she swallowed quickly and asked, "Really? Oh yeah, and he works for some IT company in Cybercity. Is his company going to be your new client?"

Nodding, Rekha explained the Softech connection and added, "And he took great joy in telling me that means I have to be nice to him." Rekha rolled her eyes to illustrate how ridiculous that idea was.

Sheela smiled and said, "So he is a prince at work, too." Then she asked, frowning, "Did he make trouble for you?"

"Oh no, Mom, it was a fairly normal meeting and we didn't even talk much. He showed us around the office and that's when he decided to be a smartass."

"Well, you let me know if he bothers you too much. I will talk to Sunita and have her set him straight." Sheela said decisively.

Rekha burst out laughing at the idea of Arjun, a grown man, being disciplined by his mother. "Mom, we are not feuding kids at school. We both have our work to focus on and I, particularly, have no time to waste on these things. We have to land this contract and that's the most important thing right now."

"Thank god, that went well." Aditya said with a sigh of relief to Rekha. It had taken two weeks' worth of work to pick a strategy and create a marketing plan, with plenty of research and fact-finding along the way. It was gratifying to see all that effort pay off. They had just presented their campaign ideas to the marketing and development team at Softech and judging by the nods and questions during and after the presentation, it had gone down quite well. There had been some questions around the budget of course, but there wasn't a client on earth who accepted a quoted fee without haggling.

After the meeting, Aditya and Rekha had been asked to join the clients for lunch. After all the hard work that had gone into the campaign pitch and the presentation, Rekha was more than ready for some food.

Sachin, Arjun and a few other guys whose names Rekha could not immediately recollect were also going to be dining with them. Rekha was too hungry to care much about that. Together they entered the continental café where delicious dishes were being served around and the muted clatter of cutlery provided a soothing background score.

Once everybody was seated, Rekha looked around and saw that Aditya was next to her and Arjun was across. Sachin was seated next to him and was engaged in a conversation with Arjun over the menu.

She had just decided on what to order, when the man seated on the other side of her, asked her conversationally, "How long have you been working with Flash, Rekha?"

"Almost five years now."

"Wow, that long? You look as if you're just out of college." He smiled when he said that, so she did not take offence. It was a common enough reaction.

Of course, her calmness was slightly shaken when Aditya piped in next to her and said, "It's because of her height. Short people always look younger than tall ones."

"Well, I don't think height's the reason for that because you tend to shrink when you get older." Rekha countered factually. She could not resist it but she had to look at Arjun to see if he had heard the conversation. She glanced up and caught his eye. Of course he was paying attention. She grinned meaningfully at him and said, "It could also be my curly hair, you know. You don't see a lot of working women maintaining curls these days."

Arjun smiled at her and mouthed 'touché'. Aditya caught the exchange and raised his eyebrows at her questioningly and she nodded to him and said "Later."

An older man, sitting next to Arjun, asked "Five years? Aren't you old enough to be married by now?"

Okay, there was idle curiosity and then there was judgement. Rekha sensed she was being judged and found wanting, and what irritated her was that she could not say "mind your own business, grandpa" to him. She had to indulge him.

"Well, marriage is a big decision and I am taking my time with it." She said neutrally and hoped that would be the end of it.

She was not so lucky.

"Time-shime." Oldie said dismissively. "You youngsters are so afraid to make a decision these days. When I was your age, I didn't have an option. I reached a certain age and it was the norm to get married. So, I did. It was very simple."

"Well, times have changed." Rekha said, gritting her teeth. Why was everyone determined to get her married off these days?

He was about to say something again when Arjun intervened and said, "That's very true, Prabhu. Just like prices have increased and corruption has risen, the risk in marriage has also become higher and that's a fact. We need to think it through carefully these days."

That got Prabhu ranting about divorce rates and he and Arjun got involved in another debate. Rekha was thankful the focus was off her because she had been about to snap. While she believed in healthy and constructive discussions and that everyone was entitled to their opinion, her personal decisions were hers alone and few people had a say in that, let alone some stranger she had just met. It also irked her that when women were making so many strides across professions, they were still expected to get married while they still could. Whatever happened to choice?

Luckily, the rest of the lunch was uneventful and once everyone had finished eating, they all stood up to leave.

Arjun came up to her and said, "And you called me a sexist pig!"

Rekha rolled her eyes and said, "Well at least he has an excuse; he is old and set in his ways. What's yours?"

Arjun frowned and said mockingly, "Oh, would you like to continue your discussion about marriage with Prabhu? I guess he's not so bad after all."

Rekha shuddered and conceded, "Alright, I guess I should thank you for taking the heat off me."

Arjun said, "Well...?"

Rekha grinned and said, "Fine, if I must. Thank you, Arjun, for reminding me again why marriage is best not rushed into."

"Hey, somehow that still sounds insulting." He protested.

"Tough! I did thank you and it's your problem if you can't appreciate it."

Arjun hesitated and said, "Listen, about the other day, when we first met, I am sorry if I was rude to you."

Rekha raised her eyebrows and said, "If?"

He grinned sheepishly. "Ok, I was rude. It's just that I wasn't sure how to say it and I was afraid you would cry or make a scene. I guess I ended up making a mess of things."

Rekha was incredulous. "What? You were afraid I would cry? Because you said I wasn't your type? Oh my god, that's right. I was devastated by your rejection and can never ever think of another man now. You've spoilt me for other men, Arjun, you handsome devil."

Arjun laughed out loud. "Alright, I guess that was a little egoistic of me. But you did ask me out and I thought, maybe, I don't know, I hurt your feelings or something."

"Well, you didn't. If I was confident enough to ask you out, I am confident enough to deal with whatever comes out of it too. Your silly notions of an ideal woman irritate me but you are entitled to your opinion." She shrugged.

"What was I thinking? Your ego wouldn't get crushed in an earthquake, as massive as it is." Arjun said wryly.

"That's like the pot calling the kettle black." Rekha retorted.

❧

Aditya was bursting with questions on the way back. "Do you know Arjun from before?" "What do you mean, he rejected you?" "I hope this won't affect the deal." The last was not really a question but more of a fervent wish.

Rekha sighed and geared up for an explanation. She had to, because Aditya had overheard a good part of her conversation with Arjun and being the conscientious account manager that he was, he had immediately become suspicious. She gave him a succinct version of her first meeting with Arjun.

Of course, her highly-edited narration did not reassure him.

"See, this is why it's never a good idea to mix business with personal stuff." Aditya sermonised.

"I didn't even realise business would be involved, Aditya. Should I investigate each of my dates for a conflict of interest with Flash, current or potential before I go out with them?"

Aditya was silent. Rekha tried to reassure him. "Listen, you obviously heard a part of our conversation; if you had heard the rest, you would have known that we are on good terms now, no harm done. Have you heard or seen anything that makes you think we don't have this thing in the bag?"

"Not so far, but anything could happen. I have to let Naveen know about this. We don't want any surprises."

"Fine, I guess if you have to, you have to." Rekha conceded reluctantly.

෬ෛ

Arjun hoped he was doing the right thing by calling Rekha on her cell phone. He had some potentially unpleasant news and he thought she would want to hear this. But he was not sure how she would react or for that matter whether she would even talk to him again.

He did not know why it was important that she like him; it was not like he wanted to impress her. He was just feeling guilty about his behaviour on their 'date' and he wanted to make it up to her. She had said she did not care about that but women said one thing but really meant something else.

"Hello, Rekha speaking." Her voice greeted him.

"Hi Rekha, its Arjun." He waited for her to say something.

"Arjun! Hello! What's up?" "Well, I don't know if you know this but I heard from Sachin that Softech has approached two more advertising companies for pitching the same work you guys are doing. He said something about the higher-ups wanting to check out the market before settling on one."

"Oh! I did not expect that. Did he mention who the agencies were?" Rekha knew this was not good. A lot was at stake, so it was natural for the client to consider the options but she was surprised Naveen had not heard about it from his friend at Softech.

"I don't know, but I will be sitting in on the presentation so I can let you know afterwards on how it went and stuff. One is in the morning and the other in the afternoon."

"That would be really good, Arjun. Thank you for doing this. It gives us a heads-up and we can at least be prepared for whatever happens."

"Hey, for what it's worth, you guys did a great job." Arjun said consolingly.

"Thanks, I think so too. But you never know with these things. You've done me a huge favour. Really, thank you so much."

Arjun was uncomfortable with that much gratitude from Rekha. "Hey, it's nothing. It's the least I could do for you know, uh, for the other day."

"Are you still on that? I told you before and I am telling you again, I am over it. It's done and dusted. Do you understand?"

"Now that's more like you, Rekha. I was beginning to feel strange with you being so nice and all." Arjun said wryly.

"I am starting to think you actually like being insulted and called names, Arjun! But however weird your ideas maybe, I owe you for this one. Thanks."

"Well, I am particularly fond of Italian sports cars, if that helps." Arjun said hopefully.

Rekha laughed at that. "I said I owe you one, not my entire life's earnings."

"Well, it was worth a shot."

❧

Rekha ended the call and thought about it. The best thing to do would be to tell Aditya and Naveen about her conversation with Arjun. Then she wondered if Aditya would blame her for this wrench. Why would he? He had been worried that her history with Arjun would affect the deal with Softech and here Arjun was the one to come through with timely and valuable information.

She wondered why Arjun had done that. As Flash's prospective client, she was the one who had to be nice to him. Maybe he wasn't such a jerk after all. He had made it clear that he was not interested in her romantically so he was not trying to impress her. It was possible that he was just feeling sorry for her like he had said and wanted to do her a favour.

That irked her a bit, because she did not want to be pitied. And she thought she had succeeded in convincing him to move past their first encounter. Then she mentally shrugged off the whole thing. There were more important things to consider other than her pride and Arjun's motives.

"I have some bad news." She said to Naveen and Aditya, a while later. They were in Naveen's office and she did not waste any time getting to the point. She told them about the projected pitch by other agencies at Softech and that the decision came from the top.

Naveen and Aditya seemed to take it well enough. At least there was no swearing.

Naveen said thoughtfully, "My friend is out of town on business for a couple of days. It seems highly coincidental that this pitch is happening just now. I wonder if somebody in the management thought that he was favouring us unduly and decided to open up the competition a little."

"Did Arjun tell you who those other agencies were?" Aditya asked.

"No, he doesn't know but he said he'll call me afterwards to let me know how it goes." She added.

Naveen said with a slight smile, "That's awfully nice of him. Are you sure he's just being nice?"

Rekha looked at them with disbelief. Men! So predictable sometimes! "No, I am pretty sure he is not this nice usually. He is feeling sorry for me because he said I wasn't his type. Didn't Aditya tell you how we first met?"

"Yes, he did. And any other time, I would be very interested to know more, but unfortunately, there are more pressing matters to handle," said Naveen. He was a little gossipy sometimes.

"That's good then. Play the sympathy card and milk Arjun for some more details tomorrow. We need to know how it goes." Aditya said matter-of-factly.

Rekha said impatiently, "I don't need to play any card, Aditya. He already said he'll call me after the meeting."

"In the meanwhile, I'll have a word with my friend, keep him appraised of this little development and see what he says." Naveen said.

Rekha did not have to wait too long the next day for the verdict. Arjun was as good as his word and called her soon after the pitching meetings. The good news was that the other two advertising agencies did not measure up to Flash's presentation and the consensus was to go with their first instinct.

Rekha was so relieved with the news that she did not even try to have the last word with Arjun.

When she relayed Softech's decision to Aditya and Naveen, both were equally elated and even suggested she take Arjun out to lunch or dinner as a 'thank you'. Rekha had a better idea—from his mention of cars and the general obsession that men seem to have with them, she had come up with a unique way of thanking him.

One of her clients in the hospitality industry had an upcoming event where the Indian entry to the Formula 1 racing championship would be showcased and a slightly modified version of the vehicle was going on a country-wide publicity tour. She had good connections with the PR manager of the hotel where the event was to take place and was wondering if she could get the F1 guys to give Arjun an up-close and personal tour.

When she mentioned her idea to Naveen and Aditya, Naveen raised an eyebrow. "That's a great idea, Rekha. You sure are taking a lot of trouble to arrange this, aren't you?" he suggested slyly.

"What do you mean, Naveen?" Rekha pretended to not understand what he was getting at. Sometimes, it was better to play dumb.

"What does it matter? It's a great idea and an excellent way to strengthen your relationship with him." Aditya said impatiently.

Rekha mentally thanked him for coming to her rescue. Sometimes Aditya's no-nonsense, business-like ways were a blessing especially in contrast to Naveen's sly humour.

In the end, it was easier than she had expected to get the personal tour arranged for the coming Sunday. Her contact at the hotel was particularly accommodating once Rekha promised her tickets to an exclusive fashion show at a competing hotel.

The only thing left to do was call Arjun. She hoped that he was free on Sunday; otherwise it was going to be tricky to get it rearranged.

"Hi Rekha, what's up?" Arjun greeted her.

"What are you doing on Sunday afternoon?" Rekha jumped in without much ado.

"Why?" He asked curiously.

"Oh, I wanted to take you out somewhere as a thank you for helping me today. Are you free on Sunday?"

"Thank you, uh? What sort of a thank you is this going to be? Where are we going?"

Rekha rolled her eyes at the volley of questions. "All I am telling you at this point is that it's going to be good. Now, are you free or not?"

"How is it that even when you are planning to thank me, you sound bossy?"

Rekha wanted to scream. "That's it, I am coming over to your house on Sunday afternoon at two and whether you want to come quietly or have the whole street watching the first ever woman-kidnaps-man story, is up to you."

Arjun chuckled. "Alright I am game for whatever you have in mind for Sunday. But only because my mother is a conservative woman and the sight of you tying and dragging me down the street might give her palpitations."

Chapter Three

As Rekha was driving her scooty to Arjun's place, she wondered what his mother would say when Arjun introduced Rekha to her. Rekha had never met Mrs. Kalyan, as she and Sheela were newly acquainted.

When she had told Sheela about her plans for that day, Sheela had given her a look of disbelief and just laughed. "I know fate has a strange sense of humour, but this is too much. You go from calling him a pig to arranging a special tour just to thank him, all within a couple of weeks!"

"Mom, as it turns out, he is not so bad. He did help me out, especially when he had nothing to gain from it. I am just giving credit where it's due, that's all."

Sheela had given her a pointed look and asked, "Are you sure that's all there is?"

Rekha snapped, "I knew I shouldn't have told you about this. God knows why everybody is making such a big deal out of it. I am just being smart and seizing the opportunity!"

Rekha spotted the house number that Arjun had given and slowed down to turn into the compound. It was a nice house, painted off-white and a pleasant green, with tall trees on the side and steps leading up to the front door.

She had no sooner rung the door bell, when it was opened by a middle-aged lady with a smiling face.

"Hello aunty, I am here to pick up Arjun. Is he ready?" Rekha asked.

The other woman looked questioningly at Rekha and asked, "Sorry, you are...?"

Didn't Arjun tell his mother what he was going to be doing that day?

"Sorry, I am Rekha, Sheela Ramkumar's daughter."

"Sheela's daughter...?" Sunita suddenly smiled and said, "Have you two decided to give it another try? Ah, this makes me so happy."

Oh no, Rekha thought, this was getting really confusing and embarrassing. Hadn't Arjun told his mother about meeting her again?

"Actually aunty, this is not about that. I work at an advertising agency and Softech is one of our new clients. I am taking him out today as a 'thank you' for some information he gave me."

Sunita now looked disappointed and confused. "Oh, he didn't mention anything to me. But then, he has always been that way." She sighed. "He is probably getting ready. I'll go tell him you are here."

Rekha made herself comfortable on one of the

A Prearranged Love

chairs and wondered about the ways of men. Despite the teasing and innuendos she had got from Sheela for telling her about meeting Arjun today, she could not imagine not telling her about everything going on in her life. Well, almost everything. There were some things that a parent just should not know! She bet Arjun would say it's because she was a woman and women just could not keep their mouth shut.

Well he was right in this case. She had a thing or two to tell him now.

❧

The moment he saw Rekha's frowning face and the look she exchanged with his mother, Arjun knew something was wrong. He just did not know what. And as a clueless male facing two females, one particularly fierce, he decided to go with the safest strategy – ignorance. They did not call it bliss for nothing.

"Hey Rekha, how's it going?" There, ultra-casual and friendly. Whatever he had done to annoy her, at least he would not be accused of rudeness.

She raised her eyebrows at that. "Why don't you tell me? Explain it just like you explained to your mom what you are going to be doing today or why I am here to meet you."

His mother was watching him and Rekha with fascination and seemed to be enjoying herself.

Now he frowned and then realised, oh yeah, his mother knew Rekha. And she was probably wondering why she was here. And he had forgotten to mention how their paths had crossed again.

"Sorry Mom, I didn't tell you before, but Rekha's

company is doing some work for us and we are going out today on business."

Rekha still looked unimpressed with his description. She looked at him pityingly and said, "Well, that's not much better but at least she won't think we are dating again."

So that's the reason for the frosty welcome this morning, Arjun thought.

"Fine, my mistake. But I didn't mean to hide, it just slipped my mind. It's not a big deal." He shrugged.

"Well, it is. That's why I made sure that I explained to my mother and yours, why I was spending time with you just so there are no misunderstandings or expectations."

"Yeah, that's because you are a woman. You folks just seem to love talking and sharing feelings and stuff." He seemed puzzled why anyone would want to do such a thing.

Rekha looked triumphant and opened her purse and took out a fifty-rupee note and put it back in again. Then she said, "I just won a bet with myself that Arjun would say 'women are big mouths' or something along that line and he did! What a great start to our day."

His mother laughed at that and Arjun knew that two women ganging up on him was not going to be a great start to his day. He said, "Is this how you want to thank me? If so, I am not going to be doing you any more favours."

Rekha seemed to remember why she was there at all and said, "Alright, we better be on our way.

It was nice to meet you aunty. Let me know if you need any help in managing Arjun."

His mother laughed again and said, "It was great meeting you too, Rekha. And I will certainly remember your special skills."

Arjun said, "Oh God, that's enough. You ladies are having too much fun. Let's get going."

He practically dragged Rekha out of the house, she led him to her scooty and handed him a black helmet.

She sat in the front seat, adjusting her helmet and checking the positioning of the rear-view mirror.

"Hold on a minute, you are driving us?" Arjun asked, with what seemed like a lack of faith in Rekha's driving abilities.

"Yes, unless you telepathically picked up the address of our destination and know how to get us there? Don't worry, I have health insurance."

"Ha-ha, very funny. Don't joke about this. I taught Mom how to drive a two-wheeler and I got nightmares the whole time."

Rekha could not help it. She pictured him waking up in the middle of the night and screaming "No!!" and that image was so funny, she started giggling.

Just when she had calmed down she saw a man and a woman, coming down the street towards them. The man was seated behind the woman, and judging from his hapless and terrified expression, was teaching her how to drive. The woman, oblivious to his troubles, did not seem to understand that driving required looking ahead. She kept turning back to talk to the man.

Rekha broke into a fit of laughter again and when Arjun asked, exasperatedly, "What is it now?" she called out and said, "Look ahead," in between her merriment.

Arjun saw what was going on and that set him off too. His deep, rumbling laughter made Rekha smile. Lost in the moment, she forgot to slow down and hit a particularly nasty speed bump on the road. Gravity forced him to bump into her and he put both his hands on her shoulders, in an instinctive need to hold something steady.

"Sorry" he said, removing his hands.

"No problem, it was my fault. I didn't slow down at the bump; I was too busy enjoying that man's plight."

"This is why I hate riding in the back. I feel like such a wuss." Arjun complained.

He definitely did not feel like a wuss, Rekha thought. When he had gripped her shoulders with his big hands, she had been startled but also strangely thrilled. She had felt small and feminine and vulnerable, which surprised her. She was accustomed to feeling petite but vulnerable? Not since she had been a little girl.

She had been disappointed when he had removed his hands and actually wanted him to continue holding her. There could only be one answer for this strange longing: she was attracted to Arjun.

Well, it wasn't too surprising. She had found him to be very attractive since the very beginning and combined with his recently discovered qualities, this proximity made for further attraction.

She had been attracted to men before, had even shared a few kisses with one object of her attraction. The man she had kissed, boy actually, had been her classmate in college. He had been cute, smart and funny. And he seemed to send out the right signals so one day, on an impulse, she had kissed him.

It had been a revelation. Neither of them had known what to do next, and though the experience was nice, it had also been awkward. At the end of it, they had pulled back, looking uncertain and walked away. Naively, Rekha had assumed that was the end of it. Unfortunately, Rohan, her partner in crime, had decided to share the little incident with his friend, who had started giving her sly looks and making innuendoes. Fed up with the whole thing, Rekha had decided to confront the two boys.

She had cornered them after class and dove straight into the matter.

"I've noticed the looks and the comments you guys have been passing lately. Is it because Rohan told you that I kissed him and you decided that gives you the right to make fun of me?"

The boys had looked surprised and guilty, and remained quiet. She had continued talking, wanting to have her say.

"Yes, I kissed Rohan. I had never kissed before and I wanted to find out what the fuss was all about.

I know for a fact that you had a crush on my friend Divya and you even asked her out on Valentine's Day. I also know she said no; did you see me going around giggling whenever you walked into a room? We are not teenagers anymore and in a few months we'll graduate and start working. How professional would it seem if you started laughing every time your boss farts or something?"

That drew a laugh from both the guys. Then Rohan said, sheepishly, "We're sorry about that Rekha and we won't do it again."

Rekha had looked at his friend questioningly. Somewhat reluctantly, he also gave his word not to behave like a juvenile teen thereafter.

But the damage had been done. She had seen the fuss created by one harmless episode and no matter how cute Rohan had been, she had realised then that women had more to lose than men when it came to flirting, dating and involvement with the opposite sex. She had been lucky that Rohan had been nice about the whole thing but what if he had been a jerk or had mouthed off about her to the whole class? She would have been branded as a fast girl and no one would have taken her seriously, including her professors.

Though dating was not as uncommon as it had been a decade ago it was still not as easily accepted as in the rest of the world and she'd decided that some things were just better left unexplored. Rekha had thanked her lucky stars for the 'wakeup call' and decided to concentrate on her grades and career.

Shaking off the memories, Rekha considered her attraction to Arjun and the potential for it to go out of hand. In this case, though, she had less to worry about than before: Arjun was not interested in her, so at least this time her hormones would not land her in trouble.

Arjun was surprised to see them entering the Hillridge, one of the ritziest hotels in the city, which got its name from the steep slope that it was perched on as well as the majestic rocks that gave it a picturesque setting.

When Rekha had refused to share details about the place they were headed to, he had assumed it was something unusual. But forget the destination; he was more bothered about the journey. What the hell had happened during the ride?

It was going alright until that speed bump. When she had jerked the vehicle, he had automatically grabbed her shoulders to steady himself. And discovered smooth shoulders and soft skin. She was wearing a short sleeved round-necked T-shirt and his unruly mind had wondered

A Prearranged Love

if the rest of her was equally soft. He had wanted to draw her close to him and crush her small and feminine body to his chest.

His instinct told him that Rekha would knee him if he were to, say, kiss her. Some women gave out 'open' vibes and some women, 'closed'. And Rekha had not given him a single 'open' vibe since the first time he had met her. Even then, there had only been curiosity and admiration in them, not the suggestive or inviting glances that some women excelled in.

After his dumb crack about her height and hair, she would probably laugh in his face if he said he was attracted to her. Not that he was going to say any such thing. He was her client; he had insulted her and said she was not his type; she had a mean spirit and god knew what she would do if pushed too hard.

So he would ignore the attraction and push the crazy thoughts out of his mind. How hard could that be?

"Well, we are here. What is this surprise that you've planned for me?" Arjun asked when they were in the hotel's sleek elevator.

"All shall be revealed soon, my friend." Rekha said theatrically.

She led him over a long carpeted corridor. When they reached room 112, Rekha rang the bell and looked at him with a mysterious smile.

The door was opened by a young, athletic looking guy in shorts and a black T-shirt and before Rekha could introduce Arjun to the other man, Arjun exclaimed with excitement, "You are Sebastian D'Souza!"

The other guy smiled and said, "I am and you must be Arjun. Come on in."

Arjun still looked a little dazed, Rekha pinched him on his arm and said, "It's not a dream, Arjun. You are in the presence of the F1 racer Sebastian D'Souza."

Arjun said 'ouch' in protest but recovered and together they entered the room.

"Would you guys like some coffee or something else to drink?" Sebastian offered.

Rekha declined and Arjun said with remarkable composure, "Sure, coffee would be good." He then turned to Rekha and exclaimed, "I am drinking coffee with Sebastian D'Souza!"

Both Sebastian and Rekha smiled at his boyish enthusiasm and Sebastian started the conversational ball rolling with, "So, Arjun, I gather you are a racing fan."

"Oh yeah, I watch every race religiously and I have been known to 'fall sick' on work days if there is a race being telecast. Your last race was so close, especially when your wheel spun during that turn in the third lap."

That got them involved in a discussion about Sebastian's finishing times and records. Rekha was amused by how little it took for two strange men to break the ice – drinks and sports.

Soon, almost half an hour had passed when Rekha looked at Sebastian and asked, "Shall we head over to the track?" Sebastian agreed and called his crew assistant for the trip.

"Tell me you are talking about the F1 circuit here when you said 'track.'" Arjun said pleadingly.

"Yes, I was." Rekha said, waiting for his reaction.

"You are a genius! How did you manage to get all this done?" he asked wonderingly.

A Prearranged Love

"I have friends in high places!" Rekha said half-seriously.

"If I had known you were so well-connected, I would have been nicer to you!"

When she raised her fist towards him threateningly, he raised his hands in surrender, and said, "Okay, don't hit, I'll behave."

They were still sharing a smile when Sebastian walked back into the room and said they were ready to go. It was decided that Rekha and Arjun would follow them to the track which was about ten kilometres away.

As they were walking towards the parking lot, Arjun said, "This time I am driving. I can follow a vehicle as well as you and I know where the track is, so no arguments, okay?"

Rekha was secretly glad that she did not have to concentrate on driving as well as ignoring his nearness so she made a show of sacrifice and said, "Fine, if you must."

The roads to the track were not as widely used as the main roads so the result was a fairly bumpy ride. Rekha was too busy gripping the bar behind her seat for support; Arjun, on the other hand, was trying to navigate the bumpy roads and not think about Rekha's proximity. But temptation took over and a wicked impulse made him break harder than usual. As a result, she bumped into him and held his shoulders for support.

"Sorry, that was a big bump." Of course he was not very sorry about the sensation of having her close by.

"It's fine. We're going to reach the tracks soon, anyway." At least that's what Rekha was praying for.

Thankfully, they arrived at the F1 grounds fifteen minutes later. Sebastian and his crew were already there and so was the fiery red model race car, decorated with the chequered flag and various other stickers.

Sebastian led them to the vehicle and Arjun had a

reverential look on his face when he stroked the shiny bonnet.

"Oh, she's a beauty." He said.

"Well, technically, this is not the car that will be racing at the Grand Prix; it's been slightly modified to travel on the local roads for the publicity tour. You want to give it a spin?" Sebastian offered.

"Would I ever!" Arjun didn't have to be asked twice.

Arjun strapped on the safety helmets and soon, was revving the engine and the sleek car rolled smoothly on the circuit.

He drove two laps and then guided the car to the pit-stop.

Arjun got out of the low-slung vehicle with a wide grin on his face.

"Did you have fun?" Rekha asked rhetorically. The grin on his face was answer enough and it just made him so heart-stopping attractive that she had to say something or remain slack-jawed.

"Man, it was awesome. I wish I could ride that beauty every day." He said wistfully.

"You and every grown man on earth, dude." Sebastian said wryly, joining them.

"Thanks so much for this, Sebastian. It's been fantastic and I am glad Arjun had so much fun." said Rekha.

Arjun chimed in with his thanks and then they said their goodbyes and got ready to leave.

When Rekha was walking back towards her scooty, Arjun called out to her to wait.

She turned and watched him come towards her with a serious look on his face.

"Hey, I just wanted to say thank you. This is the best surprise I've ever gotten and I know I'll never forget it." Arjun said.

A Prearranged Love

If a grinning Arjun was distraction enough, a sweet Arjun was too much for her senses to bear. If he continued in this vein, god knows what her crazy impulses would make her do. And they were supposed to drive back together for god's sake!

Rekha pulled herself together and in an effort to make light of it, said, "I figured I couldn't go wrong with something involving cars. I'll never forget the look you had when you saw Sebastian. I swear you had such an adoring look on your face."

Like most straight men accused of adoring another man, Arjun promptly protested and said, "Hey, I do not adore him, Okay? I just admire him for his skill."

Then he realised how that would be construed and saw the grin on Rekha's face. Rekha burst out laughing and he joined in after a mock-glare.

On the drive back, Rekha was musing on how much she had enjoyed the day, despite her ill-advised attraction to Arjun. In her line of work, she occasionally had to schmooze clients, though not as much as Naveen or Aditya did. She had always looked at it as a thing she had to endure as part of her work and sometimes an evening with a client would turn out to be more interesting than she had expected. But she was always conscious of the professional nature of these get-togethers and hence, did not let her guard down enough to relax.

Today, was a different story altogether. Maybe it was because of how she had first met Arjun or that they had a history beyond the professional setting, but Rekha had really enjoyed herself. In fact, till Arjun had asked her how she had arranged it, she hadn't even thought about her work. It felt like she was out with a friend rather than a business acquaintance.

Rekha wondered if she had gotten more than she had bargained for. On the one hand, she was happy to have made a good professional impression on him. On the other, however, she wondered if planning such a special thank you for him had made him a bit too special.

❦

As Arjun walked into his living room, Sunita came in from the kitchen where she had been preparing dinner. She smiled when she saw him and asked, "How was your day?"

"It was great, Mom! Rekha had arranged for a visit to the F1 circuit on the city outskirts and a ride on the model race car with, you won't believe this, Sebastian D'Souza!"

Sunita smiled and said, "That's very nice of her. She seems like a great girl."

"I wouldn't be so sure of that. She has a quick temper and she has threatened me with bodily harm more than once."

"You probably deserved it."

"Now she has brainwashed you too! That woman is pure evil." Arjun said wonderingly.

"Arjun, you had a good time today and met your racing idol. And she arranged all that. It doesn't seem that evil."

Arjun held up his hands. "Fine, don't believe me but you are taken in by her innocent eyes and smile. Only I've seen her true colours."

As he went to his room, he missed the satisfied smile on his mother's face.

While he was changing, his mind went over the whole day. It seemed that whenever Rekha was involved, she brought surprises along with her. Meeting Sebastian and riding the circuit had been awesome and thrilling. But the other surprise had been the surge of attraction that he had felt for her today. He blamed it on the physical proximity on the bike. And despite what he had told his mother, Rekha had really done something nice for him today. It was funny the way things turned out; he had informed her about the rival advertising pitches just to make up for his behaviour that first time. And what had she done? She had thanked him for his good deed with a super-special experience and now he felt like he still owed her one.

ॐ

The following Wednesday, Flash Advertising and Softech signed a contract for providing a year's marketing services. Rekha and the team celebrated it over lunch at Revive, an Italian eatery close to office.

She had just taken a bite of the delicious garlic bread when Aditya announced, "Rekha, clear your calendar for next Tuesday and Wednesday. Sachin called this morning and said that he has planned a two-day familiarisation visit for us to Mumbai, where their automobile client has a factory. Softech also has a branch there, which we will be visiting. Do you have anything major scheduled for those days?"

Familiarisation visits or "fam-visits" were orientation trips that provided an opportunity to learn more about a client's business by seeing their manufacturing operations and facilities. Rekha was excited at the prospect as she was a visual person and she understood better when she saw how things worked rather than read about it.

"Nothing that can't be rescheduled." She answered. Then another thought struck her and robbed some of her anticipation. "Will Sachin be coming with us or will somebody from the Mumbai office take us around?" What she really wanted to know was if Arjun was also coming along on the trip. Even though two days had passed since their trip to the racing track, the day had played on her thoughts constantly, which was very annoying. She would be working on a proposal at the office and suddenly images of his grin or the feel of his hands on her body would fill her mind.

She needed some distance from him because she felt that was the only way these inappropriate thoughts would fade.

"Sachin wasn't sure if he would be able to make it but he did say that Arjun would be able to accompany us." Aditya answered her question, without realising the impact it had on Rekha.

So much for her hope for distance! She kept a straight face but was really praying that she would be able to spend the two days in Arjun's company without embarrassing herself.

But then her thoughts brightened. At least she had an opportunity to catch-up with Nitu, her close friend of many years, who worked in Mumbai. Maybe they could meet for dinner in the two days she would be there.

"Hello, stranger!"Nitu's husky voice greeted Rekha when she called her later that evening.

"Hello yourself! It's so good to hear your voice." Rekha had always wanted a husky voice; it sounded so much more sophisticated than her own perfectly ordinary one.

A Prearranged Love

"Then why haven't we spoken for weeks? Who or what's been keeping you busy?" Nitu asked, hungry for some juicy gossip, as usual.

"Work's been keeping me busy and I thought I'd just show up and meet you in person." Rekha said, anticipating Nitu's reaction. She wasn't disappointed.

"Are you coming to Mumbai? When? How long are you going to be here? Where are you staying?" The questions never seemed to stop.

"Yes, next Tuesday, for two days and I don't know where I will be staying. I'll let you know once I know."

"That's great. I am already thinking of so much we can do."

"Down girl, I am coming there on business so I will probably only be free in the evenings. Let's go out for dinner or something."

"Oh... alright, I'll think of a good place for eating out. But I am really excited about your visit. It's been over a year since we saw each other."

"I know. In the meanwhile I do have some stuff to tell you I bet you'll really enjoy."

"Ooh, that sounds very interesting. What's it about? At least tell me that."

Rekha was amused by Nitu's insatiable curiosity and need for gossip. But Rekha could not give her even a hint because she was at work and even though she worked mostly with male colleagues, they could put women to shame with their penchant for nosiness.

"You are not going to believe my story but I can't talk now, so I'll give you all the details when we meet in person." After saying goodbye, Rekha wondered what Nitu would have to say when she told her about the whole

Arjun saga and her hormonal dilemma. It had been so long since she had felt such a powerful attraction to someone. She remembered discussing her crushes with Nitu and listening to her often wise, sometimes nutty counsel. Nitu had a laissez-faire attitude when it came to her love life. She was a "serial dater" who believed in thorough 'window-shopping' before selecting a man for life. Rekha had sometimes been amazed at the sheer number of men that Nitu had gone out with and wondered why she could not find a single man who was worth committing to.

She often thought that Nitu was not really ready for marriage and had once even told her so. Nitu had just laughed and said, "You caught me. Maybe the man of my dreams doesn't exist because I don't recognise him when I see him."

Having been on a date herself, now Rekha kind of understood why Nitu still had not found someone.

She had initially liked Arjun but he had not liked her. Then she had thought he was rude and shallow so she had written him off as a loser. Now he was showing another side of his nature, a funny, sweet and endearing side and Rekha was afraid that she was beginning to like him.

Just thinking about the whole situation made her dizzy and confused. If this is what happened after meeting just one guy, she had a whole new appreciation for Nitu's approach to love.

Chapter Four

Well, this is just perfect, thought Rekha. She was sandwiched between Aditya and Arjun, in the cramped airline seats and she was sleep-deprived and cranky because she had woken up at the ungodly hour of four-thirty in the morning to catch a flight to Mumbai.

As much as she liked travelling, she preferred it when she had good company or when she was in a relaxed state of mind. Thanks to her flighty hormones, she had neither peace nor a friend in sight. She had wanted to sit as far away from Arjun as possible but Aditya had led the way into their row so he had taken the window seat. Arjun had gestured for Rekha to precede him, saying, "I'll take the aisle seat, otherwise I have to sit hunched over."

Now she could not ignore Arjun and talk to Aditya

because that would just be rude. She cursed etiquette and Mom-instilled manners. Already Arjun had so graciously come to her rescue, when she was digging around her seat for the clasp of her seat-belt and Arjun had simply held up his hand and said, "I'll do it" and efficiently clicked the thing into place for her.

She had wanted to grab him by his hair and kiss him till the flight attendant asked them to remain seated during take-off. Only a bit of her remaining sanity rescued her; that and the presence of Aditya next to her, already immersed in the business magazine he had brought to read on-board.

She sat back, determined to make herself as small as possible and avoid any contact whatsoever with the man on her left. Thankfully she was able to push her seat back and get a little space. She closed her burning eyes and tried to relax.

Think about the meeting with Nitu this evening and all the fun you'll have, she told herself. She wondered if Nitu herself was dating anybody.

Arjun looked at Rekha, blissfully quiet, a little sigh of breath escaping her lips before they turned up a little in the corners, forming the beginning of dimples. Her eyes were closed and her head had slumped a little to the left. Somebody clearly was not a morning person. He had been concerned when he had arrived at the airport to find her unsmiling and quiet. She was such a bundle of energy and movement that he had nervously wondered if he had inadvertently done something to make her angry. He had mentally damned women and their moods.

A Prearranged Love

He had even asked Aditya if she was feeling alright to which Aditya had replied, "She's just cranky because she had to wake up early. You should see her when we work late sometimes; the next day, she doesn't start transforming into human form until after lunch!"

Arjun smiled a little when he saw her nestle deeper into the seat and give a little 'hmmm' of contentment. She really was cute, no matter what her expressions were. Her long eyelashes fluttered lightly and then rested against her cheeks. He saw Aditya shoot him a funny look and realised he had been staring at a sleeping woman. Not just any sleeping woman but Rekha. Now Aditya was going to think he was some sort of a wierdo.

"Things are quiet when she is asleep, aren't they?" Aditya asked with a smile.

"Yes, very peaceful." Arjun said, hoping Aditya hadn't gotten the wrong impression.

Arjun wondered what had gotten into him lately. Even when he had been dating a woman, he had never mooned over her like this. He dated occasionally, although there hadn't been that many lately. Women were high maintenance, needing constant care and attention. And while he liked being with them, he did not have a lot of free time except on weekends and he mostly preferred to spend them with his buddies, watching a game or playing one on his PS3.

He enjoyed flirting and had gone out with a few girls in college. But when he graduated and found a job, he had found his circle widening and his preferences changing. Also, being with a woman was energy-consuming. They never seemed to be quiet; they always wanted to know what you were thinking but they never admitted what was on their mind. If you didn't call them at least once a day, they were mad at you or thought you were mad at them. It was all very draining.

That's why it was all the more surprising that he had had such a great time on Sunday. The racing circuit was wonderful of course, but even what had come before and after with Rekha had been fun. She had this way of taking charge wherever she went and whatever she did; it was very amusing to watch because it totally contradicted her 'cutie-pie' dimples and school-girl looks. He genuinely enjoyed her company. She was very comfortable to be with, despite the strong tug of attraction he felt for her.

Just then, Rekha slumped even more towards her left, almost nestling on his shoulder. He held himself very still, not sure what to do, even though his natural instinct was to put his arm around her and pull her tightly towards him. Of course, that would not go very well with his 'stay out of trouble' motto.

Rekha just wanted to dive deep into the comfortable pillow supporting her cheek. It was warm, just solid enough and smelled appealingly familiar. Like cotton and cologne. Wait a minute, why did her pillow smell like cologne?

She opened her eyes slowly, because she had the feeling that she would not like what she saw. Aditya was grinning at her and Arjun was... her pillow. That answered the cologne question. And why she had wanted to dive deeper into dreamland. Rekha loved to sleep; and she did not need much to fall asleep. When there was a solid and familiar shoulder to rest on, well, it was no wonder she had dozed off.

She straightened and turned to Arjun and said, "Sorry about that, I kind of dozed off. You should have woken me up. It must have been so uncomfortable."

Arjun just smiled back and said, "Kind of? You'd barely fastened your seat belt before you fell asleep. But I didn't mind. It was worth having some peace and quiet." He said cheekily.

"You know what, because you were so nice, letting me enjoy my sleep, I don't even mind that you are insulting me. There, enjoy your gift." Rekha grinned at him.

For a moment, Arjun looked at her and then his gaze lingered on her lips. That was unexpected and made her feel warm and tingly. In a bid to ignore the moment, she turned to Aditya and asked, "Are we about to land? The seat belt signs are on."

Just then the landing announcements were made and that mercifully forestalled any more conversation.

Rekha was not sure what was going on. Did she have something stuck in her teeth? The kind of look that Arjun had given her was more intense and assessing. She had enough trouble dealing with her feelings so she decided not to worry about his. Everyone could just sort out their own problems!

The first day was fairly busy, starting with visits to the Softech branch office followed by the scheduled tour of the manufacturing facility. Rekha was fascinated by the rows and rows of sophisticated machinery on the assembly line and the robotic precision of the operations.

She remembered several melodramatic Bollywood movies, popular during her school days, where if the hero worked at a factory, it was a given fact that his hand or leg would be severely injured by one of the machines in the next scene. She chuckled at how far technology had come, that it could all be controlled by a set of alphabets, numbers and symbols, placed just so.

She asked a couple of questions to the operations manager about the size of the factory and the kind of vehicles that were manufactured there. Everybody loved numbers and the bigger the figure, the better the visibility. The hi-tech factory would also make an interesting background for shooting a corporate video, Rekha thought. She was taking notes as he was talking, when her cell phone rang. She did not want to interrupt the information flow so she let it ring. It went into vibration mode after two rings.

He had just stopped for a breather when her phone buzzed again. She excused herself and moved away from the group to answer it. She had a pretty good idea who it was.

"Hey, where are you?" It was Nitu, of course, checking up on her.

"Hey you! I am at this factory on the Andheri-Kurla highway. I should be done in about an hour's time. What are you up to?"

"I've taken half a day off, because I wasn't sure when you would be finished. I can come pick you up at the factory in an hour."

"That sounds good. Are you sure it's not too far away?" Rekha had heard enough stories about the Mumbai traffic to be aware that such offers should not be made lightly.

"Well, it is not close by, but since you don't visit every day, it's alright." Nitu said matter-of-factly.

Rekha chuckled and said, "I guess I'll have to be happy with that." Rekha told her the name of the factory and Nitu assured her that she would find her way.

Ending the call with a smile, she walked back to where the men were standing, still deep in conversation. Aditya looked at her and asked, "Is everything alright? Was that from the office?"

Rekha gave him a irritated look and said, "Aditya, we have only been away from the office for six hours. I don't think any calamity has befallen during our absence. Anyway, it was a personal call." Turning to the other two men, she resumed her conversation.

Arjun could not help wondering who had called Rekha. He mentally thanked Aditya for being a compulsive and nosy workaholic because he had been curious ever since he saw her face brighten when she answered the phone. Now he wondered if she was meeting another 'date' for matrimonial purposes in Mumbai. That was a bit far to travel for a date.

Of course, it could just be her mother or a friend or some such thing. How ridiculous to think she had come to Mumbai to meet a date. It wasn't even a trip she had planned in the first place. And why the hell was he so curious about a phone call?

She was driving him crazy. He was used to women paying attention to him and flocking to him and he sort of took it for granted. It was probably the forbidden attraction theory. He was trying to behave himself and not hit on her but all this restraint and good behaviour were wreaking havoc on his psyche.

He needed some time alone, just to relax, maybe with a couple of beers. Perhaps he would ask Aditya to join him for drinks in the evening. Just two guys drinking and maybe watching some sports at their hotel bar. Simple and easy, unlike a certain woman.

Soon, they finished their tour and Rekha asked,

"What are you guys doing this evening?"

He was afraid that Aditya was going to suggest something that would include all of them and he just wanted some time away from Rekha, so he hurriedly said, "I am just going to relax in the hotel. Maybe watch the cricket match at the bar. It's been a long day."

Aditya asked, "There is a match on tonight? Maybe I'll join you. If you don't mind the company, of course."

"Sure, sounds good to me." Mission accomplished. Of course, he did not want Rekha to feel left out.

"Do you want to join us too, Rekha?" he asked reluctantly.

"No thanks. I don't get cricket. Over 10 hours of play, when only the last 20 minutes matter."

Arjun and Aditya looked at each other, with an 'is she serious?' look.

"Besides," Rekha continued, "I am meeting a friend of mine for dinner. She should be here to pick me up soon, and then we'll be off."

"That's great. Have a good time." said Arjun with a relieved smile. Probably too relieved, judging from the strange look she was giving him.

"Tell me, tell me, tell me!" Nitu was half-chanting, half-nagging Rekha in the car, a short while later. She had picked up Rekha at the factory a little after four and they were now on their way towards the other end of the city, for some dinner, bargain shopping and a visit to one of the city's bustling beaches.

"Tell you what?" asked Rekha innocently; she always took some joy in tormenting her nosy friend.

A Prearranged Love

"You should know. You said you had to share some juicy gossip. C'mon, don't make me beg." Nitu whined.

"Are you really so deprived of news that you'd beg me?" Rekha asked teasingly.

"Mine is the usual stuff. Work, dating – some good, some not; it's not often that you have some news to share."

Rekha did not know if she should feel insulted or flattered. "Do I have so little going on in my life?"

"C'mon, you live with your Mom, you don't date and I am pretty sure you haven't had a crush in years, 'cause I'd have known."

"See, now that's where you are wrong, my friend. I was on a date just a few weeks back and you'll never believe, but Mom set me up on it! Ha!" Rekha said triumphantly.

Nitu's reaction was candid as always. "What? I am not sure if your Mom's that cool or you're so dorky that you'd go out with some guy your Mom recommended."

Rekha grinned and said, "Let's say that we both reached a middle ground and I decided to give it a try."

"Well, how did it go?" Nitu asked impatiently.

"It was a complete disaster. I thought he was cute, he thought I was short and not cute. So I told him I thought he was a jerk and he said I was a pushy feminist. It was a mutual admiration society all around."

Nitu chortled. "Welcome to the club; you see what I've had to put up with all these years?"

"Oh, you haven't heard the rest. No jumping to conclusions till I tell you the whole story, ok?"

"Fine, continue."

"Here I am, disappointed with my first outing in the dating world, my pride crushed and my confidence shattered forever."

"Don't overdo the drama, girl."

"As I was saying, my ego had taken a beating and I hoped to lose myself in work, especially since we had just signed on a new client. I arrive at their office for a meeting and who should be my client contact but none other then Mr. McJerky?" Rekha finished with a flourish.

"What? He was there?" Nitu took her eyes off the road and looked at Rekha to make sure she was not kidding.

"I was as thrown-off as you are, Nitu. Looking back now, it's pretty funny how that worked out but you can probably imagine my reaction then."

"What a freaky coincidence! Of all the men in the world, you run into that guy again."

"I guess it's not that odd when you think about it. Eligible bachelors, as defined by moms who want their daughters married, need to have a secure, well-paying job and Hyderabad is the hunting ground for IT yuppies. And, Softech is known to hire techies in herds."

"Oh yeah, 'trespassers will be recruited' is supposed to be an unofficial HR policy of many IT companies." said Nitu, who was a HR consultant for a global BPO company.

"Anyway, what did you do when you saw him? Did he recognise you?"

"Yeah, he was smug and annoying and I was caught in an awkward position because I had to be nice to him so I didn't explain how we'd met and pretended like I didn't know him before."

"Yeah, how would you have explained something like that anyway? Did he make your work difficult?"

"Actually, no. He, in fact, helped us secure the contract." She told Nitu how he had come through for them and impressed her boss.

"Wow, he sounds like Jekyll and Hyde, nasty one minute and nice the other. How does he look?"

Rekha grinned at that. She had expected that question a lot earlier. "You just met him back at the factory, how do you think Arjun looks?"

Nitu's mouth fell open and Rekha was thoroughly enjoying herself. It was usually Nitu who was full of stories of dating, life in Mumbai and living alone. Rekha had her share of stories, but none as dramatic. She could understand why people were glued to those daily soap operas, however illogical they were. It was nice having someone hang on to your every word.

"Rekha, you've been holding out on me! I was, in fact, going to ask you about the cutie at the factory. He is very attractive, yaar." Nitu exclaimed.

"And therein lies the problem. He is too cute and in addition to that, he is also quite nice. I am having trouble resisting the urge to kiss the hell out of him. And you know what happened the last time I kissed a guy."

Nitu dismissed that with a shrug. "That was more than five years ago. And I think you are overreacting. I've kissed a guy or two myself and when it didn't work out we parted ways without too many problems."

"But you have a certain freedom that I don't, Nitu. Mumbai is bigger and a more cosmopolitan city compared to Hyderabad. Not to mention the fact that I am crushing on a client who doesn't find me attractive. If I do kiss him and he were to react negatively, it will affect our professional relationship, and I will be ruined. And I am not even talking about my personal reputation here. If one wrong word gets out, that'll steal focus away from my work, which I am very proud of."

"Point taken. I've never dated someone from work so

I can see how that might get complicated. Why don't you try avoiding him as much as you can? Or picture him with a beer belly and ear hair; that should do the trick."

Rekha pictured Arjun with a big gut and curly hair jutting out of his ears and just burst out laughing. "If at first disgust doesn't work, try ridicule." She said in a sage voice and this time Nitu joined in the laughter.

The rest of the evening was spent reminiscing over the past and present. Rekha and Nitu had met in Hyderabad at St. Peter's College, both of them pursuing their bachelor's degree.

They had first met during General English, a course usually regarded as a 'fluff' subject balancing other main electives. Rekha had been cranky because the class was an early session and not a very interesting one at that. Her eyelids were fighting gravity and she was trying her best to focus on the notes that she was taking down and avoiding eye contact with Ms. Robel, the over-zealous English professor. Ms. Robel was notorious for starting a discussion if anybody showed the least sign of interest.

She then happened to glance at the girl at the next desk, Nitu, who was busy "air-writing" on her notepad, her arms and shoulders moving vigorously. When Rekha looked closely, she noticed a novel spread on Nitu's lap. Underneath the desk, every once in a while, Nitu would furtively flip a page with her left hand while continuing to 'write' with her right. Ms. Robel had not yet caught on to her multi-tasking because they were seated towards the back of the class.

Rekha was at once amused and irritated at Nitu's efforts to do two things at once, when she had trouble even keeping her eyes open. Nitu had sensed Rekha's

A Prearranged Love

eyes on her and when she looked up, Rekha had whispered, "You are not fooling anyone!"

Nitu's face had immediately broken into a mischievous grin, seeming delighted that someone had caught her and shrugged unapologetically. Of course, that carefree grin had sealed their friendship.

After graduation, Nitu had found a job in Mumbai as an HR assistant and had jumped at the chance to be on her own in such a cosmopolitan city. Rekha had wanted to study further before she decided on a career, so she had enrolled for a Masters in Mass Media and Communication at the local university. Unlike Nitu, she did not have 'itchy feet' and was quite happy to remain in Hyderabad.

They had stayed in touch regularly over emails, phone and in person, whenever Nitu happened to visit Hyderabad to see her parents.

No matter how much time had passed since their previous meeting, the two never ran out of topics to talk about. That night they had dinner at a busy Turkish restaurant and over a dessert of baklava and cream, Nitu mentioned something that Rekha had completely forgotten about.

"When are you going to go out on another 'date'?" Nitu asked, savouring a bit of cream.

"Date? You mean another guy who comes highly recommended by my Mom?" Rekha shuddered at that prospect.

"Come on, you've been through that once already. How much worse can it get this time? Besides, it'll take your mind off Arjun and that's at least worth trying."

"Hmm, you may have a point. Maybe it's because he is the first guy that I 'went' out with that I am so into him. You know what they say about your first, don't you?" Rekha asked with a sly smile.

Nitu raised her eyebrows at that. "I think you should seriously consider that date. Arjun is not just affecting your mind; he is also impacting your sense of humour."

"Alright, I'll do it. But I have to wait for my Mom to bring it up, you know. I can't just ask her to set me up, especially after the first time. She'll think I have gone nympho."

"Yeah, right. That'll be the day!"

They looked at each other and started laughing again. It was past eleven by the time Nitu dropped Rekha back at her hotel. After saying her goodbyes, Rekha walked up to her room and switched on the lights after stepping in. Feeling very relaxed and happy from the good food and company of the evening, she stood surveying the room and decided to hit the bed. It was past her bedtime, especially since she had an early start the next day.

After changing and brushing her teeth, she switched off the lights and crawled under the covers.

She was just falling asleep and was in that soothing phase where the mind was preparing to shut down and the body was already there, when she heard a knock on her door.

At first, it didn't register. Then she heard it again, louder this time. She got up from the bed, unsure as to what to do next. Why would anybody be knocking on her door so late in the night? Should she answer it? What if it was something urgent?

She slowly walked towards the door and after checking to make sure the lock was still in place, she asked "Who is it?" in a firm voice.

"Rekha?" followed by a tentative "It's Arjun."

A Prearranged Love

"Arjun? Hang on a minute, let me open the door."

Still puzzled, she pressed the doorknob and twisted it to pull the door back. Arjun was standing there, still in his clothes from earlier that day, looking slightly unsure.

"What's wrong? Why aren't you asleep?" Rekha asked.

"Umm, I was downstairs, having drinks with Aditya in the bar. I passed by your room and couldn't hear anything, so I thought you were still out."

"Do you need something?" Rekha could not imagine what that could be.

"No, it's almost midnight. I was wondering where you were. 'Cause, it's late, you know."

"Yes, and I am here, safe and sound. And sleepy." She added pointedly.

"Hey, I am sorry. I was just worried." He did look kind of stressed, Rekha thought and immediately felt guilty.

"Uh, its fine. Look, why don't you come in? I feel strange standing in the hallway and talking."

Without waiting for an answer, she walked back into the room.

He followed her and suddenly she did not know what to do. She had felt guilty for snapping at him and she did not want to end their conversation on that note so she had invited him in. Now, she was vividly aware that a man she hardly knew was in her room at this late hour of the night. She imagined what Nitu would say to that and then mentally scolded herself. What did it matter anyway? This was Arjun. She had nothing to worry about. She would just thank him for his concern and send him on his way.

"Do you want some water?" Without waiting for his

answer, she handed him a glass of water from the small bedside table, pouring a glass for herself too.

"Umm, sure." He took the water from her and downed it in two gulps.

"You want some more?"

"Please." He held out his glass. She poured him some more and was amused at his thirst. She had assumed the guys would have quenched it with beers. It was sort of endearing to see him chug down water like a thirsty boy after playtime.

Okay, that was not good. She really had it bad for the man, if she found the way he was drinking water cute. Think ear hair, Rekha, she told herself.

"So did you have a good time with your friend?" Arjun asked, jerking her out of her thoughts.

"Oh yeah, it was great to see her after such a long time. We've known each other since college so we go a long way back. It was a wonderful evening. What did you do?"

"Aditya and I had a few drinks and then dinner. The match wasn't all that interesting and it was getting late. You know, you should be careful when you are out late. It's not that safe for women."

"Relax, it's not like we took the bus or the local trains. She dropped me off in her car. Besides, we are both sensible and tough women. We can handle ourselves."

"Yeah, you look real tough in that night-shirt." He smiled, looking at her top. Rekha looked down and realised that she was wearing her 'Tough-Cookie' shirt; it was a buttercup yellow and had a picture of a mean-looking, choco-chip cookie, with muscles.

She could not help it; she giggled and that was a wrong move with her mouth full of water. It went down the wrong way and she started coughing and sputtering. Arjun stopped laughing when he saw her choking and quickly came to her side.

Holding on to her left shoulder, he started slapping her on the back and the shock of his hands on her body made her cough some more.

She waved her hands as if to tell him to slow down and he softened his grip and patted her more gently this time. She coughed a couple of times and he continued to hold her and rub her back. Slowly her coughs stopped and he was still rubbing her back. There was only silence and the soft glow of the room's table lamp. She was acutely aware of the thin T-shirt and the imprint of each of his fingers through the soft fabric. They were stroking her skin ever so slowly, she wondered if they would feel just as good without anything between them.

She sighed despite herself and he stopped his ministrations which jolted her back to the present.

Here he was trying to be nice and helpful and she was fantasising about him like some desperate and pathetic woman. This had to stop or else she would go insane.

Trying to recover and give away nothing of her turmoil, Rekha pretended to shrug and stretch her shoulders and used the action to move away and face him, at a safe distance of course.

"Thanks Arjun. That really helped. Although I thought the first few slaps felt a bit too enthusiastic. Saw a chance to get back at me and took it, eh?"

Arjun looked at her intently for a moment, it seemed, and then smiled and said, "It was a god-sent opportunity and to waste it would have been unforgivable. But you recovered quite fast; I would have liked a few more minutes."

"And I would have been black and blue and every colour of the rainbow from all those beatings."

"I thought you were tough, like your T-shirt proudly proclaims."

"I am all out of toughness now. It's been a long day, my sleep was disturbed, I almost choked and then had to endure barbaric beatings; there is only so much I can take."

"I guess that's my cue to leave. Have a good night's sleep. It's another early day tomorrow." He turned and was about to walk to the lift when Rekha felt compelled to say something.

"Arjun," she called him and he turned and looked at her.

"Thanks again, for coming to help me just now and for worrying about me earlier. Good night."

He looked at her, almost as if he wanted to say something else and then said, "Good night and sleep tight, Rekha."

Chapter Five

Rekha was about to use all of her excellent communication abilities and see if her mother took the bait. She was about to ask Sheela to set her up on another date.

It had been four days since the trip to Mumbai. If she did not want to tempt fate while continuing to work with Arjun, she needed to distract herself. What better way to do that than meet up with another man and see what happens?

Rekha decided two things were possible; either she would end up taking a shine to Mr. New and Arjun would be a distant memory in her mind or she could meet a total loser and with the way her life was going he would reappear in her life as another client. Of course, she would then have to give up her worldly life and become a nun.

"Mom, I've decided I am ready to go on yet another one of your 'dates'.

Sheela looked up from the TV to where Rekha, was sitting on the other end of the couch. It was just after dinner and mother and daughter were relaxing, both not really paying attention to the TV; Sheela was flipping through a magazine while Rekha was pretending to read a book.

"Hmm, I am not sure I like the scepticism behind 'date,' Sheela mimicked her daughter's air quotes and continued, "but why the sudden interest?"

"I just need to move ahead in my life. Work's been interesting but predictable. Friends have all moved away or are settling down themselves. I am wondering what's next for me. Maybe its marriage, maybe not; but it's good to explore the options." She did sound pretty convincing, Rekha thought to herself. Maybe because it was partially true. Lately she had begun feeling a bit restless. She had a good life but it was the same old good life. She had even wondered if she should pursue further studies or do research abroad but had discarded the idea because her studying days were over and she wanted to do rather than learn.

Was that why she had agreed to the date with Arjun in the first place? If so, that had certainly shaken up her life. Things were definitely not the same anymore.

"I am glad you've given this some thought. I was worried that you'd never agree to meet another man and was wondering if I would ever see you married." Sheela sighed dramatically.

"Wait a minute." Rekha held up her hand. "I said I wanted to explore the options; not get married to the next guy I have coffee with. So, no pressure, ok?"

A Prearranged Love

Sheela would have said yes to anything at that point. When it came to her daughter's marriage, things had to be accomplished not by force but with diplomacy.

Sheela was a fast worker. She had found another 'eligible bachelor' for Rekha from a matrimonial website. Rekha was amazed at how tech-savvy her mother had suddenly become. She vividly remembered a time not too long ago when Sheela had dismissed the internet phenomenon and exclaimed, "Why would I need an email account? Who would ever send me anything?"

The mystery man was a thirty-year old mechanical engineer whose name was ironically, Karan. If Hindu mythology was anything to go by, Karan would be the antithesis of everything Arjun stood for and Rekha was thankful for that at least. It boded well for the evening.

But before she could forget her troubles in Karan's company, she needed to confront them first. She had another meeting at Softech today and she was sure Arjun would be around to confuse her. But she had been good so far and if she could stay strong during the back massage in her hotel room in Mumbai, she was comparatively safer in a busy work environment. Thank god for open offices!

Arjun saw Rekha entering the lobby and could not help as a grin spread across his face. He was just glad to see her, he reassured himself. Why wouldn't he be? They got along well, she was fun, he was funny and they had not got on each other's nerves during the entire trip to Mumbai. Overall, a great working relationship.

Plus, she was soft and cuddly and her hair smelled like oranges, his unruly mind reminded him.

He was a normal red-blooded man; of course he remembered their accidental embrace in the hotel room. He hadn't even tried anything. He was just being a nice guy, helping her when he had seen her choking. Could he be blamed if he had been bewitched by the curve of her back and the gentle slope of her spine and continued to rub her, even after she had recovered her breath?

That was just a momentary impulse. And he had been a perfect gentleman afterwards. So if he was happy to see her now and had in fact, sort of, volunteered to bring her up from the reception, that did not mean anything. He just liked her as a potential friend.

In fact, to prove that he thought of her as a friend, he was going to invite her to watch a movie with him. Like friends do.

"Hey Rekha, how is it going?"

"It's been good. How about you?"

"Not bad, either."

Wow, Arjun thought to himself. They hadn't had such an awkward conversation even on their first meeting. How did he hope to impress her with such scintillating banter?

Wait a minute, why did he want to impress her? She was just a potential friend, right?

Impatient with his self-examination, he decided to bite the bullet and said, "I wanted to watch Sherlock Holmes at the multiplex this evening. Do you want to come along?"

Rekha seemed surprised at the offer and asked, "This evening?"

"Yes, have you got plans?"

Rekha hesitantly said, "Yeah, I really wish I could go. I wanted to see it too. Heard it's really good."

Arjun seized the moment and said, "Then come with me. You can do whatever it is tomorrow."

"I can't." Then she sighed and said, "I am actually meeting a guy, you know, like on a date...."

Arjun was so taken aback by that, he did not know what to say. He must have looked surprised because she went on to explain in more detail. As if that would help things.

"My Mom set me up for this and I thought, you know, it might be worth trying out. After all it can't be worse than the previous..."

She did not get to finish what she was saying because Arjun could not stand it anymore. He dragged her towards a quiet corner, ignoring her questions, grabbed her shoulders and did what he had been wanting to do for a while now.

He kissed Rekha.

He wanted to keep it light because he just wanted to see how it felt and also, confirm whether she felt any attraction for him.

But once he felt those soft lips, her citrusy scent and feminine warmth enveloped him and all thoughts of confirming were forgotten. It was with great difficulty that he remembered what he was doing, not to mention the fact that she might knee him any minute. He slowly pulled back and looked at her.

"Wha...What... was...that?" Rekha asked faintly. She felt a surreal atmosphere embrace her. A part of her was appalled at her poor response and quivery faint voice. She sounded like a blushing maiden from a Barbara

Cartland novel, for heaven's sake. And there was the other Rekha that was actually blushing, hopefully only on the inside, who was shocked out of her mind that Arjun had kissed her and still felt the imprint of his lips on hers, remembered his embrace and how good she had felt.

"Wow, I guess that's one way of shutting you up." Arjun said with a grin.

Oh, he was going to play it all cool, was he? Well, two could play that game. Time for the wimpy virgin to take a hike and the tough chick to come on stage.

"Try that again and you won't be walking for a week." She threatened.

"I didn't notice you protesting then."

"Well, you pounced on me like one of those predators on Animal Planet. And I was taken by surprise. One minute, we were talking about going to a movie and the next minute, you are kissing me."

"Predators? You don't need to use force, Rekha. Your words alone would bring an army down." Arjun said dryly.

"Serves you right. Don't you know it's rude to cut somebody off when they are talking?" Rekha grinned at him.

He grinned at her and then remembered what she had been saying before the kiss. He frowned and said, "Do you really want to go on that date tonight?"

He was being direct so Rekha decided she owed him the same. "I only agreed to that because I thought it was time to give dating another chance." She didn't tell him she felt compelled to distract herself with another guy. There was no need to give his already healthy ego another stroke. Besides, she still did not know why he had kissed her or where she stood with him.

"You still haven't answered my question." Arjun said.

"That depends on why you asked." She wasn't giving an inch.

"Isn't it obvious? If you're so eager to try dating, why don't you try it with me?" He challenged.

Rekha looked at herself up and down. Then she grabbed a strand of her hair and mock-checked to see how it looked. "Arjun, I don't know how to tell you this, but I haven't grown any taller since our date and my hair is still as curly as noodles." She said regretfully.

Arjun had the grace to look sheepish and Rekha knew she should not be so petty but she could not help feeling smug.

"Fine, I am sorry I said those things. I don't know what I was thinking; clearly I don't know myself very well and despite your smugness, your sharp tongue and grouchy morning personality, I think we should, you know, try getting to know each other." He looked irritated at having to spell everything out. Such a guy, Rekha thought to herself, amused.

"Well, I don't know Arjun. I am not sure you are my type." Rekha wasn't about to let him get away with his back-handed way of admitting his feelings. Grouchy personality, indeed!

"Oh really? Well maybe, we should test it out. Why don't we try kissing again?" He advanced towards her threateningly.

Rekha was now truly in a quandary. She was eagerly anticipating kissing him again but at the same time, wanted to prove that he did not have such a powerful effect on her.

Pretending nonchalance, she said, "Fine, if you must."

Arjun smiled at her knowingly and backed her

towards the wall. He placed one hand on the wall, on either side of her and bent his head towards her. She closed her eyes in anticipation and held her breath. Everything seemed to be suspended in motion and she swore she could hear her heartbeat. She felt his lips on her eyelids and opened them in surprise.

"Don't worry; I am pretty sure I am your type." He said, looking into her eyes.

She felt flustered with his intent gaze and said "We need to get going. Sachin will be waiting for us." She slipped from under his arms and strode away quickly.

"Rekha," Arjun called out to her.

"What?"

"The meeting room is to the right, you know." He said with a smile in his voice.

She glared at him and turned the other way.

She did not know how she got through the meeting. She did not remember anything about it afterwards. She tried not to act different and focused on treating Arjun with professional courtesy. She must have been successful because everything went on as normal and their discussion was mercifully brief.

Afterwards, she tried to slip away quickly; she had not made a decision about meeting Karan yet. She did not want to cancel on him at the last minute, but she was not looking forward to meeting him. She had only arranged the date because she wanted to forget Arjun; of course, if she had really wanted to forget him, kissing him probably wasn't a good idea.

And what was she going to tell her mother? Sheela was surely going to ask questions regardless of the outcome of the evening. But Rekha felt uncomfortable even contemplating dating another man when she had somebody else on her mind. Her thoughts were in such turmoil, she wasn't even sure she would be good company.

But slipping away was made impossible by Arjun who insisted on seeing her out and she could not very well refuse in front of Sachin.

"So what's it going to be? Movie with me or a boring date?" Arjun did not waste any words.

Rekha felt like she was being held at gunpoint. "Look Arjun, I want to go to the movie with you. But I asked my mom to set me up with Karan and it'd be rude to ditch him like this. Not to mention, dealing with the questions from my mom."

"So you're going to date him out of politeness?" Arjun challenged.

"I am not gonna date him at all. I'll meet him today, make some awkward conversation and tell my mom we didn't have anything in common. And we can see a movie on Friday, alright?"

"Fine. But make sure you don't lead him on. Just be brutally honest with him."

Now Rekha was offended. "Excuse me? Did you just imply that I was a tease?"

"Of course not. But you know guys, go out for a coffee with them and they may get ideas and start imagining stuff. You never know." Arjun shrugged.

"Thank you, Dr. Freud. Seeing that you are such an expert on human behaviour, you should know that women don't take very well to being ordered about by men they barely know."

"Alright, alright. I wasn't ordering you around, Rekha. I was just concerned about you, that's all."

Rekha gave him a condescending look. Typical

domineering male. But she had bigger things on her mind.

"And I don't want to let anyone know we are going to a movie, okay?" Rekha said.

"Why not?" Arjun seemed puzzled.

"Do you really want to tell our moms and have them planning our wedding and selecting names for their future grandchildren?"

He blanched. "Oh man, I hadn't thought of that."

"Obviously. We're just getting to know each other and I don't want to deal with other people's expectations. And let's not forget; you are my client and I don't want people speculating on our relationship."

"I am glad you said that. Let's just see where this goes. No commitments, etc." He looked like he was gaining his colour back.

Karan turned out to be a nice guy, albeit unremarkable. Or maybe it was because Rekha had Arjun on her mind. Karan did not make fun of her, or insult her nor did he make her laugh. He was just a nice, ordinary, non-offensive guy. Perfectly pleasant looking too. Above average height and a little on the lean side. He just did not provoke much of a reaction from her. She was not even sure that she would remember his face two days later. That irked her a little bit. Was she going insane? Did a guy have to treat her badly for her to be attracted to him? She wondered how she would have reacted to Karan if she had met him first. Would she have dismissed him as boring or considered him interesting enough to give him another chance?

What did it matter now anyway, she asked herself impatiently. She was seeing Arjun the day after tomorrow. A part of her was sort of nervous, wondering what she had agreed to. Yes, things had started off on a bad note between them, but it had gotten better since then. His touch and kisses made her feel funny, warm and very aware of herself.

But she did not know how things would be now that they were 'seeing' each other. She had seen her girlfriends in relationships. Suddenly life was a big drama; if the guy did not call one day, the girl started dissecting every word exchanged and every gesture made. Then came the sulking and making him pay, followed by the making up.

She wondered if dating made a woman turn all needy and emotional. She shuddered to think that the same might happen to her. Being with someone you like should not make you feel so unsettled.

And now she had the inquisition to face back home. But Rekha decided to be charitable about that. She had asked for it after all. So she would just have to face the music.

"Where are you off to? You're packing up early." Arjun was caught off-guard when one of his co-workers asked him about his plans on Friday evening.

"Oh... just catching on a movie with a friend. The latest Sherlock Holmes one." Good save, he congratulated himself.

"Lucky you. I still have this module to test and that's sure to take another hour at least." his colleague said with a long face.

"Too bad. I've gotta run. The show starts soon." He knew he did not sound too sympathetic. He worked long hours himself and that was an occupational hazard in the IT sector. However, he had more pressing things on his mind today.

He was still surprised Rekha had agreed to go out with him; and lest he forget, she had kissed him too! Not that he was insecure about his appeal. He knew he was an attractive man and he never had trouble with women or spending time in their company. He had always been outgoing with a good sense of humour and interest in a lot of things, so he did not conform to the myth of the 'IT nerd'.

But from the beginning, he had never known where he stood with Rekha. She did not react the way most women he knew would. And she made him laugh at the most unexpected times. He still could not believe that he had told her on her face that she was not his type. That itself was proof that she confounded him.

Never mind all that; he was seeing her soon, in a dark theatre and intimate setting. His mind was already imagining all the intriguing possibilities.

The evening did not go exactly as he had expected. There they were, seated in the reasonably full hall, popcorn in one hand and drinks in the cup holders. Arjun's interest was partly on the screen and partly on the woman next to him. She was bent down, fiddling in her giant purse for something; why did women carry such huge sacks? How did they ever find anything in there?

"What are you looking for?" Arjun asked curiously.

A Prearranged Love

"Just my handy-cam; gotta get a good angle to ensure a good print for the film. My clients don't like skewed frames."

She looked up at him and burst out laughing. "Oh! I really wish I had a handy-cam; anything to capture the shock on your face." She snickered again, recalling his expression. Someone shushed them from behind.

He could not resist it. He turned and hooked one of his fingers in her curls and tugged her closer.

"I wish you had a handy-cam, too. The look on your face is pretty."

"Yeah, right. Like you can see anything in this darkness." She challenged.

"I can feel the heat on your cheeks." He retorted.

"OK, lovebirds! Some of us want to watch the movie! Do you mind?" said an annoyed voice from behind.

That got Rekha snickering again, which led Arjun to shushing her, followed by a few more shushes. It was like a wave formation. For a moment, the hall felt like a giant tea kettle, with all the hissing and whistling.

Arjun decided the wise thing to do would be to step outside for a few minutes to regain their composure.

He stood up and pulled her outside the hall. She laughingly followed him. When they were outside, they just happened to see a poster for a horror film on one of the walls; it had a picture of a finger held up to blood-red lips with the word, 'Shhhhh'. They looked at the poster and then at each other and then burst out laughing again.

"I am not in the mood to see a thriller movie now." Rekha said suddenly.

Arjun thought about it and agreed. "Why don't we do something else? Do you want to go up? They have a gaming arcade." They took the escalators to the second level and the moment they stepped out, Rekha's face brightened.

"Oh, foosball tables! Let's play!" Rekha rubbed her hands together in anticipation.

"Are you sure? I am very good at foosball. I don't wanna make you cry on our date."

"We'll see who cries and who crows soon enough. What say we make it interesting?"

Arjun raised an eyebrow. "Keep talking."

"The winner can ask the loser to do anything, even stuff that they don't like. But only once, OK?"

Arjun smiled wolfishly. "Are you sure? That is very broad. I could ask you to do anything."

"And so can I. Something really pleasant like watching two hours of a soap opera and writing an essay on it's salient features."

Arjun cringed at that. "Fine, you are on."

The next hour was filled with the click-clack sounds of the wooden players banging into the ball and the occasional triumphant cries.

It turned out that Arjun had not been exaggerating when he had said that he was good. He beat Rekha by one point and Rekha could barely stand all the crowing that ensued.

Foosball was followed by dinner — spicy Mexican food at the food court and before they knew it, it was almost nine. Arjun insisted on dropping Rekha home and since she had enjoyed the evening so much, she did not protest too strenuously.

Rekha was not too sure what the proper date etiquette was, but deciding to be honest, she looked at him and said, "Thanks Arjun. I really enjoyed myself. Despite missing the movie, I had a great time."

He looked amused and said, "Nice try. You're not getting rid of me so easily."

A Prearranged Love

It was either the night or the man, but suddenly feeling emboldened, she said, "Oh fine, why does it always have to be the woman's job to do this?" Saying so, she grabbed Arjun by the shoulders and did what she had wanted to for a while.

Not being a man to miss a golden opportunity, he grabbed her by the shoulders and Rekha leaned in even more and kissed Arjun with enthusiasm.

Arjun seemed surprised by her initiative and then, emboldened by her response, stroked her lips with his tongue; she was so surprised by his move that she let him slip his tongue inside.

At first, the kiss seemed strange and too intimate. But Rekha slowly relaxed and it helped that Arjun kept it light and gentle. She tasted him, a little bit sweet and a little bit salty. She vaguely thought that even his taste matched his personality. Belatedly she remembered that she was kissing a man outside her home, where anybody including her mother, could see her.

She opened her eyes and stepped back, literally and mentally. She looked back towards her house, checking for prying eyes.

"Now you have to leave."

"Fine, toss me aside, now that you've had your fun with me." Arjun mock-pouted.

God! Even that looked sexy on him. "Do you want to come in and say 'hi' to my mom? I bet she would just love to meet you." She was being sarcastic and hoped to scare him.

"Why not?" He shrugged.

"I was kidding! You are not coming in to meet my mom. Didn't we agree that we weren't going to say anything to anybody?"

"Listen, who did you tell your mom you were going to the movie with?"

"You, of course."

"Then, wouldn't it make sense if I meet her casually when I drop you off? Isn't it more suspicious if I skulk away in the shadows?"

She pictured him tip-toeing in the dark like Jerry, the mouse and grinned realising he did have a point. "Fine, come on in. But keep it short."

He sighed. "You make me feel so loved."

If Sheela held any hostility towards Arjun for rejecting her daughter or suspected any hanky-panky going on, it did not show when she greeted them.

"Did you enjoy the movie?" she asked.

Rekha was taken by surprise and hesitated a bit when she replied. "Oh yeah, it was very good."

Arjun added helpfully, "The tone of this movie was very different from the previous adaptations."

Rekha raised her eyebrows at him. What, had he read the reviews? She had to admit that was a good move.

"Really, in what way?" Sheela pursued the topic with interest. Clearly 'adaptation' was the magic word.

"Uh, you know, because the previous movies were sort of serious and sober, whereas this is, um, very light-hearted and stylish." Arjun managed.

"Sounds interesting. I should watch it sometime."

"Oh yeah, it's worth a watch, Mom. In fact, I'll watch it again with you." Just in case Sheela saw it and came back with points for discussion. Arjun really should have quit when he was ahead.

A Prearranged Love

Rekha glared at him and then looked at her watch pointedly. He got the hint.

"Well, it was nice meeting you aunty. Bye Rekha."

"I'll see him out, Mom."

When they got to his bike, Arjun said, "You are very welcome, you know, for saving you."

"Saving me? Because of your overacting, you almost gave it away. Different tone, ha."

"Hey, that part's true. That's the trick to lying, Rekha. Prepare and stick to the truth as much as possible."

She blustered, "Fine, master, I bow to thee. Now, goodnight."

"What? No kiss goodbye?" He caught her look and knew enough to take a hint.

❧

"He seems like a nice enough guy. Such a shame he is not interested in you." Sheela said wistfully.

"Well, that's all old news, Mom. We get along well now." Rekha was in a hurry to distract Sheela from the current topic. She felt guilty for having to lie to her mother about what had, essentially, been Sheela's idea. But it was a big enough change for her to start dating someone; she did not want to deal with parental expectations and to be honest, she wasn't sure where she stood with Arjun. Yes, he was interested in her now. But he had not been before and he had been around the block a few times.

"So things could change?" Sheela persisted.

"Oh, what does it matter? We work together now and maybe in a few months, once that's over, we may not even see each other very often." Technically that was all true, Rekha consoled herself. Although the thought of not seeing Arjun again was unsettling, like a bright spark extinguished.

She had just come back from her first real date with Arjun and now she was feeling sad as she contemplated not seeing him anymore. She was acting like a drama queen already. This was what she had been afraid of. She needed to change the subject.

"What were you up to today?" She asked Sheela in an attempt to distract both of them.

"Oh, I went shopping with a colleague from college. The new Garewal store at M.G. Road has some great discounts. You have to see what I got!" Grateful for the reprieve and brightening at the thought of seeing her mother's loot, Rekha followed Sheela, her dating troubles temporarily forgotten.

Chapter Six

The next week was busy for Rekha. She had two or three advertising campaigns that were about to go live so she had to work on the final proofing, get approvals and sign-offs from the client and coordinate with the print and electronic media.

Also, she had deliberately avoided calling Arjun. There were three reasons for that. One, she did not know whether she would be assuming too much if she called him. They had been on one date and they had both agreed on a 'no-strings-attached' policy. Two, she didn't know what the proper dating protocol was. Did one allow a suitable time to lapse before one arranged another date? Something similar to a mourning period, perhaps? Equating dating to dying was rather morbid, Rekha thought, amusedly. The last and decidedly selfish reason was that she needed some distance from him.

From the beginning, well almost, she had enjoyed herself around him. He was smart, funny and easy to be with. And that had been before he had kissed her. It was one thing for her to be attracted to him. It was maddening and embarrassing but she had only her feelings to worry about. But now that she knew he was as attracted to her, it was a bit overwhelming.

Thoughts that were strange came unbidden to her now. For instance, this morning, she had stood in front of the mirror, wearing traditional clothes, a green and blue chudidar kurta instead of her usual formal shirt and trousers. Then she had wondered what Arjun would think of her outfit. Did he, like all men, love blue? And did he also prefer women in traditional wear over trousers? She had been surprised and appalled at herself for caring. She had always dressed to please herself and her moods and had never given a thought to what somebody else might think, especially a man's opinion.

If this was the side-effect of one date with Arjun, could she withstand more? She felt unsure and confused, as if she was driving in the dark with her mirrors fogged up. She desperately needed a manual she could refer to or a standard operating procedure that prescribed a set of rules for dating.

Two more days passed this way and she stuck to her vow. Luckily the fact that she did not have to visit Softech that week helped. She was winding up her work on Friday. It was three in the afternoon and several of her colleagues were filling in their weekly reports and other paperwork.

She was debating whether to give Arjun a call and suggest another movie. That seemed casual enough and would serve to reopen the lines of communication. God, to hear her talk, it sounded like she was beginning a hostage negotiation!

She was mentally rehearsing what she would say when her phone chirped. Something told her it would be Arjun and it was. She could not control the smile that spread on her face. Answering the phone, she said, "I was just about to call you."

There was silence on the other end and she wondered if her vision had played tricks on her and it was not actually Arjun calling. Then he said, "I was wondering if I had done something to piss you off again."

"Why?"

"It's not like you to be quiet for so long!"

"Do you want me to get mad at you?" she huffed.

He laughed. "How are you?"

"I am good. And you?" They sounded like two old, very polite people who were meeting after a long time.

"I am okay, had a busy week at work. That's why I couldn't call you." He sounded apologetic.

Rekha was surprised enough to respond, "That's okay, Arjun. I had a busy week too and thankfully it's almost over. I wanted to call you and see what you are doing tomorrow. Are you free?"

"Sure, what do you have in mind?"

"I was thinking we could go see a movie, you know, actually see a movie this time?"

"Sounds good. What do you want to watch?"

"You are leaving the choice to me? Don't you know that's dangerous?"

"Why? You are not gonna make me watch some chick-flick, are you?" He sounded a bit unsure now.

Despite herself, she laughed. Talking to him was so

energising. She felt so alive and always curious to hear what he would say next.

She suggested a movie that she had wanted to watch. It had one of her favourite actors in it and the story seemed promising.

He groaned at her suggestion. "Oh no, I can't stand him. He overacts most of the time. Do we have to?"

"Alright, you suggest something then."

Predictably, he mentioned a recently released 3D feature with lots of special effects and, Rekha suspected, little or no plot.

"Ugh, why do guys like that one so much? A couple of my colleagues were raving about the graphics. I prefer my movies with flesh and blood acting."

"Fine. How about this? Let's meet up and decide what to watch. Be impulsive. How about Megaplex at eleven?"

"Alright. See you tomorrow."

Rekha hung up with a smile. All of a sudden, the ambivalence about Arjun was not there anymore. She had not felt awkward about suggesting that they meet again and he had been eager to agree. Belatedly, she remembered that she had lost a bet with him that involved her doing something he liked and they were going to watch a movie in a dark and intimate setting. No wonder he had agreed so quickly.

Arjun knew that Rekha was not like the women he had dated. But he was still surprised when, after not speaking for almost a week, he had called her and not only had she not been chilly or angry, she had been pleased to hear from him and seemed to want to spend more time with him. In his dating experience, if he had not called at least once a day, he had known he would face some sulking or tears at the other end. Why had she not been upset?

Maybe she was even more diabolical than he had expected and was planning to exact her revenge in person. It was a testament to his questionable mental state that he was still looking forward to tomorrow.

The next morning, he relaxed slightly when he saw her smile and wave at him from the wide stairs at the entrance to Megaplex. She was wearing a white and red churidar-kurta and a small black bindi. She looked so pretty that he could not help exclaiming, "You look great today, Rekha!"

She grinned back at him and said, "Thanks. Admit it, you may say you want a modern woman but you'd rather look at a women dressed traditionally than a woman in trousers, wouldn't you?"

He cheerfully admitted, "Yup, it's the old-fashioned Indian male in me but there is something about a woman in a saree that brings out the inner beast." And he let out a little howl like a werewolf.

She was still laughing at that when he looked at her and said, "So you really aren't mad at me."

She didn't understand the sudden change in conversation and said blankly, "Uh?"

"Most women sort of expect a guy to call them every day so when I called you on Friday, I was wondering if you would be mad because we hadn't spoken."

Rekha wondered what he would say if she told him that she was sort of relieved that he had not called because she needed the space. She bet he would be offended. Nobody wanted to hear that. But it wasn't because she did not like him; it was because she liked him a bit too much.

Since she could not explain herself truthfully, she decided to play the outraged feminine card.

"You thought I was so needy and girly that I would go all crazy stalker on you?! After one date?"

Belatedly he realised that he was caught in a quicksand and like any sensible guy, he retreated.

"No, no, not at all. I was just curious, you know. But I should have realised you are different."

Rekha was amused and relieved at the direction of the conversation so she said, "And don't you forget that!"

Since he was in an appeasing mood, he relented on their movie decision and they ended up watching Rekha's pick.

An hour into the movie, Rekha was caught up in the story and the romance, as well. There was something so memorable and satisfying about watching a well-shot romantic plot. When a particularly intimate scene was unfolding on screen, she felt the heat rolling off from the screen. She was curious to see how Arjun was reacting. When she turned to look at him, she saw that he was looking at her and even though it was dark, she could feel the intensity of his gaze and felt audacious enough to hold it.

He grabbed her hand resting on the arm rest between them, raised it to his lips and kissed it. Instinctively she turned towards him and he leaned in and closed the rest of the distance. Sinking low on his seat, he was so close to her that she felt his warm breath on her cheeks. For the moment, the scene that had captivated her attention just a few moments before was completely forgotten. So were the people surrounding them. There was only her and him. He nuzzled her cheeks and she felt his lips close to her ear. Around the lobe. Then he gently bit her lobe. She was so surprised by the exquisite sensation that she gasped and then shivered delicately.

She felt more than saw the woman sitting in the row in front of them turn at the sound she had made. Both embarrassed and amused, she pretended to cough and then told Arjun, "I am alright now, so it's okay."

She could feel Arjun's questioning eyes on her and she pointed her finger to the lady in front of her. Arjun caught on quickly and said, "Are you sure? Maybe I should thump your back some more."

She could barely keep her face straight when she said, "Oh I don't think so. I barely survived the last time."

Arjun leaned close to her and whispered, "Honey, you ain't seen nothing yet."

"Oh, you're so cheesy!"

"Admit it, you were all turned on."

"Shush Arjun! I want to finish watching this movie at least."

With a look that said he fully intended to continue the conversation later, Arjun turned to face the screen and let her watch the rest of the movie. Of course, after his earlier shenanigans, she could barely remember the movie's plot; her brain was scrambled and her senses were in a whirlwind, not giving her time to assimilate anything. Thankfully, Arjun decided to keep his hands to himself but she could not escape his presence next to her.

Since they had the rest of the afternoon to themselves, once the movie was over, Arjun suggested they go to a nearby park. Even though Rekha did not want their time to end, she aired her objections to his idea.

"A park? That is such a cliché! And so tacky. You know, when I used to walk in the park and see all those couples hiding behind a bush, I would laugh at them!"

"Would you rather go to yet another coffee shop, order an overpriced beverage and try to hear each other over loud music? It's such a beautiful day."

Rekha accepted his argument. It was a great day to be outdoors, not too sunny and a light breeze was tickling her curls.

The park was about a kilometre from the movie hall and they decided to walk the distance rather than take either of their vehicles. Since it was Saturday, the roads were not as crowded so they could walk at a good pace and enjoy the relative peace of the day. They had to cross the road at one point and Arjun gripped her left hand while looking both sides for oncoming vehicles. The gesture was so unexpected, it took Rekha by surprise. While the independent spirit in her rebelled a little at being made to cross the street like a child, another part of her thought it was subtly romantic and tender.

Of course, then he had to go and ruin the moment. When they finished crossing, he nudged her to the pavement side of the street and said, "Walk on my right so you are away from the traffic."

She snapped her fingers and said, "Yup, now I know why the feminist movement took shape."

He frowned at her and said, "C'mon, you can't seriously have a problem with that. I am just being considerate."

"And yet your species rarely remembers birthdays and special occasions, doesn't clean up after itself and are bad listeners."

"And your species uses their wiles to their own advantage. You say you don't want special treatment but you'll expect men to give up their seats for you in the bus or train. And call them pigs if they don't."

"That's because we are tired of being groped and pinched by men while standing. Not to mention losers falling all over you when the driver breaks!"

"If women speak up when that happens rather than keeping it all bottled up inside, we would actually get somewhere."

"So it's our fault for not wanting to make a scene?"

"Well, you shouldn't complain without having the courage to stand up for yourself."

Rekha started to get annoyed and then she remembered – she actually agreed with him and had frequently debated with her friends using the same arguments.

She held up her hand and said, "Hang on, I agree with you."

He looked at her blankly.

She laughed and said, "There is something about arguing with you that really gets me going! My first instinct was to say something contrary before I remembered that we shared the same view."

He shook his head and said, "You're nuts."

"Maybe so, but you are here with me so you're equally crazy." She smiled.

They had reached the park's arched entry and Rekha was thankful that it was too early for couples to take refuge under the shady trees. They saw a few people, mostly old, taking an afternoon stroll or chatting on benches.

They chose a bench, a little away from other people.

Rekha deliberately sat a little away from Arjun. She still felt weird doing the very thing that she had teased her girlfriends mercilessly about.

Stretching back, they were both admiring the greenery without speaking but it was a companionable silence. The park was sort of circular, with an old fountain in the middle. Tiny yellow flowers surrounded the fountain and the entire view was very charming.

Rekha was once again marvelling at how nice the day was when Arjun asked suddenly, "I know I am going to be risking all kinds of feminist wrath but I have to ask. Have you ever kissed before?"

Rekha smiled and bemusedly said, "I am not sure what brought that on. This park isn't even all that seedy."

"Well, you refused to come here and you have this air of, reserve I guess, that says 'I am not open' so I just wondered."

Rekha was quite surprised. She had expected and feared that since she had kissed him, he would assume that she was easy with all men.

He must have mistaken her silence for reluctance to answer so he said, "It's okay Rekha. It's actually quite refreshing that this is all new to you. Dating has become so common these days that many think it's a necessity."

Rekha did not know whether to be amused or irritated; irritated that he automatically assumed she was a prude and amused that he was speaking as though he was a wizened old man.

She put up her hand and said, "Stop. I have kissed someone before and you just sounded like a know-it-all."

He was clearly taken aback.

"I hesitated because I wasn't sure if it's a good idea to discuss exes."

"I will if you will." He promised.

"You might really regret saying that."

"Oh, just confess. Did you really kiss somebody?"

She told him the story of her first kiss, obviously editing some for etiquette's sake.

He listened and then looked at her consideringly. "So you started the kiss, huh? Who knew that such a wild soul existed inside such an innocent exterior?"

She told him the rest of the incident; the consequences of the kiss that made her wary about her impulses thereafter.

"Well, Rohan was just being a guy, you know." He said defensively.

"So you've done it too?"

"If you are a guy and especially, if you are sort of new to all this, then a girl laying one on you is a big deal. Don't tell me you girls don't share everything about your life."

"Oh, the big difference is we are subtler. We don't let anything show."

"Fine. But there is one thing I don't understand."

"What?"

"You have even more at stake now than you did when you were in college. I am your client and yet you agreed to go out with me. Was it because you couldn't resist me?"

Little did he know, Rekha thought to herself. He had driven her so crazy with mad impulses that she had been afraid she would do something she would definitely regret later. It had been sheer relief when he had taken the wind out of her sail by making the first move.

But of course, she was not telling him that. He had such a big head already. So she went with a believable half-truth.

"There are three reasons for that. First, we met even

before you were my client. Second, I have already told my colleagues about our history and I have been with Flash for a long time so they know and trust me. And third, I know karate."

At that he looked offended. "For heaven's sake, I am not gonna rape you!"

She shrugged and said, "I know. The karate was in case you blabbed to people about us going out."

Scowling at her he said, "Enough with the threats about bodily harm. Nobody buys that."

It was his smirk that did it. She reached out to the fleshy part of his upper arm, took a tiny bit of skin and twisted it like a door knob.

"Oww, stop that." He shook his arm and she let go. "That hurt like hell!"

"I know. A little trick I learned from a cousin of mine. Turns out that it hurts more if you take a pinch rather than a dollop." She couldn't help but grin, looking at him rubbing his arm.

"You have a big mean streak!"

"Little old me? Nobody would buy that." She mimicked his tone.

"You know what I noticed missing in your list of reasons? The fact that you trust me to stick to my word, because I am such a nice guy."

"Haha, you are funny Arjun."

He said more seriously, "You don't think I am nice? I called and alerted you about the rival pitches and then called you again to tell you how it went. I was concerned for your safety when you were out late at night when we were in Mumbai. And I was there to save you when you were choking. It makes me feel like there is nothing I can do to make you happy."

Rekha was a little disconcerted by his earnest expression and wondered if her playfulness had hurt his feelings. "Arjun, c'mon I was just kidding. Of course I think you are a great guy. I wouldn't be with you here otherwise. I even made out with you in the theatre for god's sake!"

He laughed wickedly and said, "And that's how you get women to do whatever you want!"

"Jerk!" Rekha raised her fist to punch him in the arm when he caught it and turning it over, he stroked each finger till they unclenched like a slowly opening shell. The way he was looking at her made her heart race and wonder what he was going to do next. He kissed her palm and gently bit the fleshy part of her palm and she sighed. She could not help it, she just sighed. She felt a little thrill from his move. She wanted to kiss him and feel his warm body against her. But she hadn't lost all of her inhibitions. She wished they were alone so she could do what she wanted but she was also somewhat relieved that they were not.

But she wanted to do something to him. Let him not get too sure of himself. He found it hard to believe she could be wild. Well, she'd show him! She had seen in movies where the seductress would lick her shiny red lips in a slow motion and that would have the hero salivating after her. She had not worn lipstick, just some lip gloss which had long since worn off. But it was worth a shot.

She held his eyes, smiled a little and slowly licked her lips. She thought about doing it twice just to drive the point home but decided that would make her look parched not sensual. She smiled victoriously when she saw his eyes widen a little and follow her lips. A mischievous impulse made her blow him an air kiss, the kind that beauty queens and sultry sirens on screen had patented and said, "And that's how we get men to do whatever we want."

He said, "You totally have my support to do that any time you want."

She grinned and admitted, "When I pictured myself doing that just now, it looked slurpy rather than sexy. I just don't understand men!"

"Well, we are complex and enigmatic."

"My ass! You are all horny dogs!"

She was still thinking about that little seduction scene and smiling to herself when she reached home. She walked inside and was about to call out, "Mom! Where are you?" in a sing-song voice when she saw that Sheela had company. Sheela was chatting with another of her friends, Priyadarshini and they were both seated on the sofa.

"Hi aunty, how are you?" Rekha asked with a smile. She had known Priyadarshini for a long time and was quite fond of her. Priyadarshini reminded her of her mother, with a mischievous, sharp sense of humour quite rare for a woman her age.

"I am doing fine. Did you have a good date with your boyfriend?"

Rekha was shocked for a moment and then recovered after remembering the other woman's cheeky sense of fun.

"No, he says he is leaving me for you!" Rekha retorted.

"Oh, enough, you both! I can't believe I am with two adolescents, only both of them are past that age." Sheela said with exasperation.

"C'mon we're just having fun. It's been a while since I met Rekha. What's going on with you these days?"

"Nothing much, Aunty. Work's good and I went to Mumbai a couple of weeks ago and met a friend of mine. Just saw Hrithik Roshan's latest movie today. It was quite nice." Rekha saw no harm in adding that last bit. 'Stick as much as possible to the truth,' she remembered Arjun saying. "She went to the movie with Arjun, you remember that boy?" Sheela added helpfully.

Rekha hated to side with Arjun but sometimes she wished women weren't so chatty. Apparently Sheela had told her friend everything.

"Do you two like each other again?" Priyadarshini asked eagerly, like a hopeful matchmaker.

"Well, we have become friendly. It helps to be on good terms with a client, you know." Rekha hoped that was the end of it.

She was not so lucky. "Well, if they are friends, why don't you start the marriage talks again, Sheela?" Priyadarshini probed persistently.

"Mom, no! Just because we are friends doesn't mean I want to get married to him." Rekha protested.

"I don't understand kids these days. They like someone but they don't want to get married. They say they are just friends. Who says you shouldn't be friends with your husband or wife?" sighed Priyadarshini.

"Aunty, there is something called chemistry. You can like somebody but have no 'chemistry' with them and you can have lots of chemistry with someone but can't stand him or her." Maybe she was digging a deeper hole for herself but Rekha could not help but defend her generation. Of course, she wasn't talking about herself. She had tonnes of chemistry with Arjun and she liked him. But she just wasn't ready to confess anything to Sheela. Rekha imagined trying to explain the idea of 'readiness to commit' to Priyadarshini.

Leaving the ladies to their chatter, she went to her room. She was changing her clothes and removing her earrings when she remembered Arjun kissing her lobe. She could not quite believe that she had been so intimate with him today. She had never trusted any man enough to even imagine herself with one. Maybe that was why she had agreed to meet a guy recommended by her mother! If that wasn't safe, what was?

That next morning, she woke up, a little bit shaken. She frowned and looked around herself, slightly relieved to see the reassuring and familiar surroundings of her room. She had had a strange dream. She could not remember the details except that disturbing sensation of pain, despair and abandonment. She could recall being dragged through the streets by a horse carriage of some kind. She could not remember who was driving the carriage, except that it was a man. The most unsettling part was that she could have let go of the vehicle but clung to it, letting it drag her even though it was hurting her and no one noticed it, not even the man in the carriage.

She wondered what Nitu would have to say about her dream. In fact, she was pretty sure Nitu would have a field day interpreting that one. She had such a rich source material. Abandonment – Rekha losing her father at a young age; her clinging to the carriage perhaps meant her increasing attachment to Arjun. Or maybe she was afraid of four-wheeled vehicles and that is why she had Tanya. In spite of herself, Rekha smiled at that. With traffic the way it was in Hyderabad, she had every reason to be worried about driving.

Meeting over the weekend for a movie, lunch or dinner soon became a pattern for Rekha and Arjun. Either she would call him or he would call her and they would make plans. It was not a conscious decision but a very convenient one. They both had work over the week and sometimes they ran into each other at Softech but a lot of Flash's work at this stage involved approvals so that was done through emails or over the phone. Rekha normally did not go out during weekdays because she often worked late and did not like staying out too late in the evening and worrying Sheela.

If her mother was suspicious of the growing 'friendship' between Rekha and Arjun, she did not say anything; at least nothing more than the studiedly casual questions that mothers thought were innocent. A part of Rekha was feeling increasingly guilty about not being completely honest with her mother. And even if she wanted to confess, what could she say? She was not sure about where she stood with Arjun. She did not know if she was in love with him or wanted to marry him. She really liked him and the chemistry was more than evident, but how did one know if one was in love? Maybe this was just infatuation with their constant interaction adding fuel to the fire.

How much did she know about Arjun anyway? Yeah, he had a job; he was a nice guy who was funny, cute and smart. Sometimes, she felt as though she was seeing the best side of him; so far she had not discovered anything seriously irritating about him and that just made her suspicious.

It was not like she wanted to get married tomorrow, but she did want to get married eventually and hopefully to a guy that her mother liked and approved of. However, she did not want to get married based on just a 'crush' and have regrets later. It was easy to view someone that you liked with 'rose-coloured glasses' but what if you married them on a whim and then later realised that you can't spend the rest of your life with that person?

Out of all the decisions she had to make in her life, marriage was probably one of the most important. She did not want to make it based on a fancy. And she hadn't even considered it from Arjun's perspective; he had not said anything about his intentions; in fact they had carefully not made any commitments and even during the course of their dates, neither of them had put their cards on the table. Rekha herself was so unsure about their relationship. She could not, in all fairness, expect her mother, however modern her thinking might be, to understand or accept her relationship with Arjun.

More time, Rekha thought, that was what they all needed.

Chapter Seven

The next Saturday, Rekha got what she wanted. Sort of. She and Arjun were tired of the same routine, so they decided to try something new. There was a go-karting course about 20 km from the city and it supposedly had a nice lake nearby with boating facilities and an attached resort. When Rekha came up with the idea, Arjun immediately agreed and it was decided that he would pick her up.

The ride to the resort reminded Rekha of the earlier ride to another race track that she and Arjun had taken. She remembered how jolted she had been by the intimacy of sitting behind him, the warmth of his body just inches away. It was funny because she still felt the same tension and warmth even though they had kissed a few times, as well as the episode in the park. Of course, now she did not have to worry about making a move and embarrassing both of them. However, she still could not be so brazen as to snuggle up to him, leaving not even a millimetre between their bodies.

She had always scoffed at couples who did that on motorbikes, wondering how the guy managed to drive in a straight line when his girlfriend had such a stranglehold on him. Rekha did not want to plaster herself against Arjun; that would be too suggestive, not to mention dangerous. But the distance between them was silly and she was holding onto the safety bar behind her when it would be much more convenient to hold onto him. So she gently slid her hands on to his shoulders.

She felt him laugh and when she leaned forward and asked him why he was laughing, he shook his head and just said, "Later." It was just as well because she could not hear very well with loud horns blaring all around them.

An hour later, they had reached their destination. Rekha could see the welcoming arch of the resort but what really drew her attention was the lake she could see across the grounds. The water was a pale blue colour, with some ducks swimming in it. It was not very large but the bright sun, the blue waters and the surrounding greenery certainly made for a very picturesque setting.

As they got off Arjun's bike, Rekha questioned him.

"What were you laughing about earlier?" she asked.

He looked at her and smiled. "You were sitting away from me as if I had the plague and I was tempted to brake suddenly, just to have you bump into me 'accidentally.' Of course that was before you finally gave into my manly charms."

"And they say women are devious."

They walked to the reception to enquire about go-karting and Rekha was curious to find out if they could go boating on the lake. She was a sucker for water sports and a good swimmer too.

The lady behind the reception eagerly nodded and said, "Yes, we do have boats on the lake. You'll have to walk in through those doors and turn right along the trees." She pointed to the elegant wooden doors to her side. "It's a ten-minute walk from here. To the left is the go-karting track."

Rekha was eager to get to the track but her growling stomach reminded her that she had woken up late and hence skipped her breakfast.

She nudged Arjun and said, "Let's have something to eat first. I am hungry."

"This is why you never bring girls along for an adventure. Always worried about food or water or toilets or getting tanned."

"I am too hungry to care about your insults. Gimme some food!"

She dragged him through another set of doors that had a sign proclaiming 'Restaurant'. She had noticed that right away; food was one of the basic needs after all.

They walked into a hall, decorated in rustic chic that seemed to be the go-to-theme for resorts these days and selected a table. They had a lot of choice because it was not very full; there were two or three families seated and to the far side of the hall was a gang of people about their age.

They sat down and Rekha started to read the menu. Halfway through the entries she lifted her eyes as she heard somebody call out, "Hey Arjun!" Both of them looked up and saw that it came from the gang of young people.

Arjun looked up, smiled and waved back. "Hey guys!" He got up and gestured to Rekha to join him as he walked to their table.

Rekha was feeling quite ravenous and sighed at the interruption. She noticed that Arjun's friends had already ordered what looked like heaps of food and were in the midst of eating. Then she realised she was staring at the food rather than the people when Arjun began to make the introductions so she quickly raised her eyes; she did not want his friends to think she was a pig.

They were a gang of five men and one woman. They were all dressed casually in jeans and T-shirts except for the woman who was wearing a kurta over her jeans. Out of instinct, Rekha smiled at the woman first before saying 'hello' to everyone. The woman smiled back and looked at Arjun curiously.

"Guys, this is Rekha, a friend from work. Rekha, these people are my co-conspirators way back from college." Arjun finished smoothly. Rekha was quite impressed with the 'friend from work' line. The man really was quite good at fibbing. She wasn't entirely sure if that was a good thing.

The woman, whose name was Shalini, smiled at Arjun and asked in a not-so-casual tone, "So what are you doing with a work friend on a Saturday?"

Rekha thought Shalini was being a smart ass. Deciding to be a smart ass, in return, Rekha said, "Oh, just trying to collect some medicinal herbs that are only found here. Arjun and I are volunteering at a homeopathy clinic in our spare time and this herb could potentially cure cancer."

She heard a suppressed snicker next to her. She deduced it was Arjun. Shalini looked taken aback at first and then looked at Arjun for confirmation. Arjun's expression of barely controlled glee probably gave it away.

"I am impressed. Your story was more believable than Arjun's 'friend from work.'" said Shalini which Rekha thought was a bit too personal, especially since she did not even know Rekha.

"Are you one of those who believe a man and a woman can't be friends?" demanded Rekha.

"Only if the said man and woman come to a secluded resort on a weekend." That was definitely personal. Could she be a pissed-off ex-girlfriend of Arjun's?

"Actually we came because I wanted to try the go-karting course here and Rekha asked if she could come along. Just like you with your gang." Rekha was glad when Arjun joined in. She was quite irritated at Shalini's nosiness.

One of the guys chose that moment to offer helpfully "We are different. We don't think of Shalini as a girl!"

Shalini did not take that well. She frowned and demanded, "What exactly do you mean by that, Arvind?"

Arvind looked like a fish, mouth hanging open. Belatedly he seemed to realise what he had implied and decided to change tactics.

"I stand corrected. Since you guys are just friends, why don't you join us? We were also going to try go-karting after lunch." This was said with a perfectly sincere face.

Sure, that's how I want to spend my day, Rekha thought to herself. Half starving and constantly dodging questions from nosy, possible ex-girlfriends. But she could not very well be rude and say 'no'. She was not sure if Arjun wanted to spend time with his friends either, but she had seen the excitement on his face when he had spotted them. She could do one thing.

"That's not a bad idea. We haven't even ordered and I am starving, so we'll have a quick lunch and meet you at the go-karting tracks." Rekha prayed that Shalini or Arvind would not suggest that they have lunch with the gang. She needed some time alone with Arjun. Thankfully he seemed to agree with her suggestion and that settled the discussion.

When they were back at their table, Rekha pounced on him. "Are they always like that or do I just bring out the best in people?" She asked sarcastically.

He pretended to consider that and said, "Well, you certainly brought out the best in me the first time we met."

"Careful, I am very hungry and not too happy either." Rekha raised her fork at him threateningly.

"Put the weapon down, Attila. They are nice people, just being their usual curious selves. It's been a while since we all met up and they want to know what I am up to, that's all."

"Are you sure that's all it is? Shalini seemed a bit too quick to judge us."

"She was right, wasn't she? We aren't just friends 'hanging out.'"

"That doesn't matter. It's not her business or anyone else's. Unless it is?"

Arjun did not seem to understand what she was getting at, so she explained, "She is not a former girlfriend, is she? That would explain why she came at me like that."

Arjun looked at her in disbelief and laughed out loud. He continued to laugh so hard that his shoulders shook with the effort and his face turned red.

Rekha took that to mean that the possibility of him and Shalini dating was ludicrous, which relieved her, but no way was she going to admit that out loud. Also, she wondered if like a typical clueless man, he only saw what he wanted to see – so they had not dated but maybe Shalini had feelings for him, which were not returned or even noticed.

"Are you done?" Rekha asked tolerantly.

His laughter had slowed down to occasional snickers and he nodded and dabbed his eyes with his napkin. "You girls are such drama queens. So you meet a girl who you don't click with immediately. Can't she just be someone you need to know better before you judge?"

'Maybe...' she said. Then she persisted. "Tell me this. In all the time you have known her, have you introduced her to your other girlfriends?"

"Yeah, a couple of times."

"And what was her reaction?"

He shrugged impatiently. "Oh, who knows? I don't observe people like they are under a microscope and I am not one of those touchy-feely types." He shuddered, just imagining the possibility. At her warning look, he continued, "All I remember is that she didn't become best friends with any of them."

Rekha said "A-ha!" triumphantly. "Maybe she didn't like any of them because she likes you and wants you for herself."

"Oh, you are insane. Shalini is not the type. She is a guy-guy, you know? We like her exactly for that reason." He mimicked in a high voice, "She is not like 'Do I look fat in this dress? Uh, I am so fat. Oh god, look at me, I am so dark, I knew I shouldn't have gone out in the sun."

Despite herself, Rekha giggled. He was being an ass but he was so funny and she had actually known girls like that.

Their conversational route changed and then Rekha remembered how hungry she was and she blamed Arjun for that state. They quickly ordered and thankfully their food came without testing their patience too much.

After lunch they dutifully followed up on their promise to Arjun's friends and went to the go-karting track. The others were already there; some of them had already completed more than one lap. As they approached the flag-off point, one of the guys suggested they have a race. As there were eight of them, they decided to split into two teams of four. Their times would be added up and the team with the best average would be the winner. Rekha loved a good game so she was on board.

She and Arjun ended up on the same team with two other guys. One guy in their team listed out the ground rules – you could block somebody's way and slow them down but you cannot directly bump into them. Arjun rubbed his hands together and said, "What's our strategy going to be?" Rekha raised her eyebrows and said, "What is this? Survivor?" The guys looked at her solemnly.

Rekha raised her hands and said, "Oookay, just having some fun." Jeez, they took their game quite seriously.

When the 'strategy' discussion was over, they all fitted their helmets onto their heads and sat in their karts. The attendant sounded a shrill whistle and they all took off. The guys zoomed ahead and Rekha was very amused by their enthusiasm. There were tires stacked up on the sides, to prevent accidents and nasty bumps she supposed. She saw that she was one of the few lagging behind but the day was so beautiful and the kart's momentum created a cool breeze—she did not want to rush. She drove at a decent pace and passed by the serpentine route, which went up and down. When she completed the lap, she drove towards the side so she would not be in the path of the drivers behind her.

She looked up with a smile and removing her helmet, got out of the low vehicle. Heading towards her team, she said by way of greeting, "That was fun!" The guys had their heads bent together, looking at the paper with their times on it.

"You should have driven faster. Why did you go so slowly?" Arjun demanded.

"Umm, I was going at a decent pace. I wanted to enjoy the clean and spacious road. How often do you get to drive in the city on a road like this?" Rekha replied.

"Well it's a race, not a long drive. Our team's average is down because of your time." Arjun waved the paper around.

"I wanted to have fun, so I drove the way I wanted. It's not like it's a national championship or something. So relax, okay?" She smiled as a sign of truce.

Arjun continued to glare at her, which began to irritate her. Sensing a rise in tensions, one of his friends tried to pacify him. "Don't worry, man. They have Shalini on their team and she was quite slow. I am sure we'll even out. Let's go see their times." He practically hustled Arjun away.

She watched the departing figures in disbelief. Has she taken part in the same race that they had? It was just a game, for heaven's sake.

"Nutty, aren't they?" Shalini said from behind her.

"That's an understatement."

"Ooh, you haven't seen the worst. Once we were

playing cards — rummy, and I was the dealer. I accidentally started by dealing to the wrong person; since everybody was busy chatting and looking at their cards, nobody saw it at first. When the time came to drop, Arjun realised it. He got annoyed and everybody started insisting that I deal again. I had to deal the entire pack and they were watching me like hawks this time and telling me, 'drop it here,' 'the cards are getting mixed up!' They almost drove me to tears."

"Tell me you cheated in that game. Just a little... just for the pleasure of seeing grown men sulk."

Shalini laughed. "Well, I was tempted but I took the high ground."

Rekha groaned at that. "They are idiots!"

"Thanks, I think so too. You heard Arvind earlier; apparently I did so well at not being girly that the guys think I am a boy with boobs." She said sarcastically.

"Do you want them to notice you that way?" Rekha asked seriously.

"No, it's not like I want them to make a pass at me or something; that would be awkward. But once in a while, it would be nice to be treated like a woman. I can't remember the last time any of them told me I looked nice or did something thoughtful for me." She said wistfully.

"I know what you need!" Rekha said as something occurred to her.

"No! Please, 'not the ugly duckling turns into a stylish swan' routine. I have read 'Pygmalion' and liked it but I am not gonna dress differently just to get a little attention. This is not a Hindi movie."

Recollecting those films where all a heroine had to do to get the guy was dress like a femme fatale, dance around and have the hero be smitten by her in just a song, Rekha felt for Shalini. But that was not what she had in mind.

"Don't worry, I wasn't gonna say that. What I meant was, you should hang out with your girlfriends more. The support of the sisterhood. When you ask if you have gained weight, a gal pal always says 'no, you look the same.' She is not annoyed if you have to go to the restroom to straighten your hair. In fact she'll come with you. She'll go shopping with you and be as anxious as you are to find the perfect shoe."

"You sound like an advertisement for girlfriends."

"It just so happens that I am in advertising. But seriously, don't you sometimes feel like spending time with your female friends? I am more comfortable in women's company, to be honest."

Shalini looked thoughtful. "Hmm, I don't have that many girlfriends. It's just that when you hang out with a particular group of friends a lot, you kind of lose touch with others. I do have a couple of colleagues at work who are girls. I work in IT, by the way."

"Wow, another techie. What do you do, exactly?" Rekha asked curiously.

"I am in networking, I work for Volance Consultancy."

"Oh yeah, in Phase 2 at TechCity, right?" Rekha had often passed by their offices on her way to Softech. Almost all the big players in IT were working out of TechCity.

"Yes, it's a nice place to work. Maybe I should socialise more with my workmates. I don't want to end up like Elaine Benes, with only obnoxious or downright strange men for friends."

Rekha grinned at that. She loved a good TV reference. "That'll teach these guys not to take you for granted."

Shalini grinned back and then turned serious. "Listen,

I didn't mean to be rude earlier, when Arjun introduced us. The guys were getting on my nerves and then we saw Arjun with you and I assumed you both were being coy about just being 'friends'... I guess I just needed an outlet."

I was right, Rekha thought to herself. She had told Arjun that Shalini had snapped for a reason. Of course, she had assumed that was because she was annoyed at seeing Arjun with another girl; little had she known that Shalini had her own problems, hardly related to Arjun or her.

Rekha had probably taken it a bit too personally because she was the guilty party there. Arjun and she weren't just friends who were out together. But she did not want to admit anything to Shalini. She felt that would ruin her credibility altogether and their newfound camaraderie, especially since Rekha needed a friendly voice, now that Arjun and the 'boys' were mad at her for making them lose.

She looked across at the guys and caught Arjun's eye. She smiled, signalling a truce but he did not return her gesture. Okay, she was done being the bigger person. She did not understand Arjun. He had seemed so light-hearted and easy-going. She could not believe he was taking this silly game so seriously.

She was lost in her thoughts so she did not immediately realise that Shalini was speaking to her.

"Let's go find out who won. I feel like we are at war with the guys and I don't want to ruin the rest of my day."

That sounded like a sensible plan to Rekha so she walked along with Shalini.

"Hey guys, which team won?" Shalini asked in a cheerful voice.

A Prearranged Love

"We did, by about 87 seconds. Isn't that great?" Arvind said triumphantly.

"Well, the important thing is that we had fun." Rekha said.

"That's what people who lose say." Arjun said mockingly.

"Maybe they are just being a good sport instead of being all insanely competitive."

"Or maybe just plain lazy."

"Guys, just take it easy. We are here to have fun and not ruin our day. So what shall we do next?" Shalini tried to change the mood of the crowd.

It was assumed that Rekha and Arjun would be joining the others and for that she was very grateful. Imagine being stuck with Arjun when he was in such a sour mood! Just thinking about it made Rekha cringe.

In the end, they went boating on the lake. Well, boating was an overstatement. The lake was the size of a tennis court and it had little wooden boats designed like ducks bobbing on the water. The guys cringed when they first got a look at their sailing vessels but probably to keep the peace, gave in and got into them. Each duck-boat seated two people and there were just enough to accommodate all of them.

Rekha paired up with Shalini and the boat operator briefed them on how to pedal and cast off the boat. They had to sail by pedalling and continuously steering with a wooden handle bar–which was in front of the boat. Rekha sat in the front and when she looked at the yellow pedals shaped like duck feet, she had to laugh.

"This resort seems to have a duck fetish." She remarked to Shalini.

Soon they were bobbing away. It took more effort

than Rekha had expected. But it was nice being in the water and taking in the scenery.

Since it was a small lake with only four crafts in it, their paths were bound to cross. The girls' duck grazed one of the other boats and Shalini laughingly urged Rekha to bump harder. Rekha even saw Arjun smile a little. Thank god for small favours, she thought.

Their antics in the lake lasted well over an hour and it was past six in the evening when they were done with their fun and games. Rekha half-wished they could linger awhile because she really did not want to face Arjun alone. He seemed to have thawed a little but still had not said a word to her.

Goodbyes were said while Rekha and Shalini exchanged numbers and promised to be in touch. Rekha and Arjun walked towards the parking lot in silence. He handed her the helmet and she took it wordlessly. Rekha did not want to be the one to start a conversation; she had already had her efforts snubbed. She even went back to gripping the bars behind her for support.

The drive back seemed to take forever, probably because the atmosphere was not as light as before. When he stopped the vehicle in front of her house, Rekha was glad to be home. The day had been upsetting and fun, in unexpected ways. She looked at Arjun and said, "Thanks Arjun. Good night." He may sulk but she wasn't going to let that ruin her manners.

She was about to turn and walk away, when he called out, "Rekha, wait."

She turned back, not sure what he had to say now that he could not have said earlier. She did not say anything and just looked at him. She was not going to lay the groundwork for him.

"Did you have a nice time with my friends today?" he asked.

Rekha raised an eyebrow in disbelief. "That's it? You don't speak to me most of the day, except for making snide comments and now you want to know how I feel about your friends?"

"You weren't a good sport, Rekha. You just wanted to do your own thing."

"What? I am not a sport?" Realising her voice had gone squeaky with outrage, Rekha willed herself to calm down and continued in what she hoped was a level voice.

"I went along with it when you said 'let's join my friends' even though I didn't know them at all or even liked them much. I went along with it when you said let's race. In fact, you are a bad sport and a sore loser."

He frowned and retorted, "We wouldn't have lost at all if you had kept pace with everyone."

Rekha lost it. "Oh my god, enough with the race already! It was just a freaking race. Do you even realise how silly this is?" Her voice rose again and she hated yelling almost as much as she hated being yelled at.

"Oh, so it's silly that I wanted you to support me?" he demanded.

"But it's just a game." She didn't understand why he was taking it so seriously.

"Maybe to you but not to me! You don't even understand that."

"Why didn't you just tell me how important it was for you? I don't take these things so seriously."

"It's a race, Rekha. We play to win. Didn't you see how the others were doing?"

"That's the thing. I didn't pay attention to what the others were doing. Why should I? Why would I?"

"You know what? You won't get it. Good night." He put on his helmet and started the engine.

"Wait, don't leave like this." Rekha felt frustrated and lost. And now he was going off without having reached a truce. It was different when he had been sulking. Rekha had felt righteous because she had made an effort to reach out, but now, he seemed disappointed and maybe even hurt.

Soon all Rekha could see was the fading twinkling of his bike lights and she stood staring at the street long after he had left. Now she wished she had said sorry or something else; anything that would have killed their fight and more importantly, that look in his eyes. It was as if he had expected something of her and she had failed him.

A dog barked in the next street and the sharp noise brought Rekha back to her surroundings. She had been standing there for a while and would probably be questioned if Sheela saw her now.

She walked into her house and removed her shoes. Thankfully Sheela wasn't around to ask questions or chat. Rekha's expression would have given her away and she was not yet composed enough to pretend everything was fine.

She went to her room to change and wash her face. She looked at herself in the mirror and all she could see was the look on Arjun's face.

She had heard from friends and even experienced it herself. A fight never started from big or serious issues. It erupted from the silliest of things and took a shape that was, in retrospect, ridiculously out of proportion. She felt like calling Arjun and doing whatever it took to set things right. But then a small part of her desisted the very idea.

She did not even know why he was mad at her. Well, that was not strictly true; she knew, she simply did not understand. Now that they were dating, was she automatically supposed to go along with whatever he wanted? Or was it that she simply did not know how important it had been to him. In which case, was she just expected to read his mind? The whole thing seemed way too complicated to her.

Since thinking about it seemed to bring on a headache, and she needed a distraction, she changed her clothes and went to find her mother.

Sheela was in the kitchen, preparing dinner and Rekha decided to give her a hand.

"I am back! What are we having for dinner?" She asked.

"I am making puris. Come, I will roll the atta and you fry them." Sheela said, handing her the slotted stainless steel spoon. She proceeded to roll out small, circular pancakes out of the wheat dough. Rekha watched with her usual fascination. She had often asked her mother how her puris were always so perfectly round, no matter how many or how quickly she made them, like some sort of Fibonacci sequence for culinary science! And they puffed up so well and evenly, it was an art.

"You are unusually quiet; didn't you have a good time today?" asked Sheela.

Rekha did not feel like faking cheer, so she said, "Well, it started out nice; we met Arjun's friends and decided to try out go-karting. Then Arjun got all mad because I was driving slowly and our team lost the race because of that." She was aware of how accusatory she sounded.

Sheela laughed. "Men!"

"You think it's a male quality? Taking these things so

seriously?" Rekha asked curiously. That put a different spin on things. Here she had been thinking maybe it was an Arjun thing or maybe she had not been a 'good sport'.

"Well, I know more competitive men than women. Your father used to turn into a crazed version of himself when there was a cricket match on TV. Once, there was a crucial game between India and Pakistan. It was the final over, I think. He was so obsessed with it that he wouldn't let me move the remote. He insisted that I shouldn't touch the thing because it would bring bad luck."

"You're kidding!" Rekha said in disbelief. She had early memories of her father, of impressions and feelings. For instance, whenever she smelled neem, she remembered him because he had always bathed with neem soap. As a child, she had always thought of him as 'dad' and not someone with quirks or oddities.

"So did we win the match?" Rekha asked fondly.

"No, we lost by four runs because our players didn't have the confidence to go big. Of course your father insisted that our argument had created bad vibes and that's why our team lost." Sheela laughed.

Rekha laughed too and felt a bit relieved. Arjun was just being a guy, irrational and obsessed with sports. She had not been insensitive or hurtful. All was well. Tomorrow, she would call him and no, she was not going to apologise; she still thought he had acted silly. But she would make the first move and get things back to normal.

She was half tempted to ask her mother how she had handled her dad when he got into one of his 'zones'. But that sounded a bit too 'woman-to-woman-asking-for-advice-on-man-problem' and she did not want to raise any suspicions. The heavy feeling in her heart was gone and she dropped another puri into the oil.

Chapter Eight

The next day, Rekha waited impatiently to finish work. She wanted to call Arjun and did not want to give him an excuse of being at work to avoid her call. Of course, he could still choose to ignore her. But she wasn't the one to give up. She had some things to say to him and he was going to listen to her, one way or another. So she waited until after six in the evening to call him.

When the phone went unanswered for a while, she thought of hanging up and trying again later. But after seven rings, he finally answered.

"Hello?" He said brusquely.

Rekha smiled to herself. He was clearly playing hard to get. "Hi, what are you up to?" she asked casually.

"Nothing much. Work was busy."

Not sulking but still not quite his usual funny, cheerful self.

"Can you talk now? If you are busy, I'll call later."

"No, now is fine."

Rekha took a deep breath and said, "I got the feeling yesterday that you were disappointed in me because I didn't support you in the race. I'll always support you and would have done yesterday too if you had just let me know how serious these things are for you."

"So it's my fault for not telling you how much everything means to me?" He said defensively.

"It's nobody's fault. That's what I am trying to say. I don't take things like sports so seriously. I am sure there are some women who do but I am not one of them. Now, I wouldn't expect you to remember girly things like the colour of the dress that I wore the first time we met etc. So if I wanted you to for some reason, I would tell you how important it is to me so you'd understand too. Are you still mad at me?"

"That depends on what you might do to get me to forgive you."

Rekha let out a relieved chuckle. "There, that's the Arjun I know and lo-like." That was close! She had almost said love, probably because that's how the phrase went but imagine if she had said it out loud. Would that have freaked him out?

"Seriously, my feelings are still hurt, you know. I might need you to pay a special visit and make me feel better."

"Said the Big Bad Wolf to Little Red Riding Hood! Nice try though, I'll give you an 'A' for effort. I'll just have to make it up to you this Saturday."

"Hmm, a whole day of penance? I can come up with a thing or two that will heal the hurt." He said mischievously.

"Alright, that's enough free passes for the day. Get your mind out of the gutter and I will see you later. Okay? Bye."

"Bye, Rekha."

Smiling, she hung up. There, that wasn't too hard. This was another reason why she was so drawn to Arjun, apart from his obvious attractions. She felt so comfortable with him, whether they were arguing or just indulging in banter, she never felt at a loss for words or bored. Unlike some of the girls in her college, she had not mastered the art of flirtation and the few times she had tried it, she had groaned because to her own ears it had sounded lame.

But now look at her! Trading barbs and innuendos like a femme fatale in a James Bond movie. Love really brings out the hidden side of people, she mused. Wait a minute, love? That was twice now; how innocent had that earlier slip of the tongue been? Did she love Arjun? Was that why his hurt had upset her? How the hell does one ascertain these things anyway? She was confused. Quick, she told herself. Imagine kissing another guy. A really smart, funny and hot guy. She closed her eyes and tried to do so – the only guy she could visualise was Arjun.

She decided to run through her laundry list of qualities that she wanted in a partner. If she called him up anytime she was in trouble, would he come? He already did, remember, her mind reminded her. Did he respect women and their independence? Yeah, he was protective sometimes but he had never dismissed her work or her views. Good kisser? Check. Would he be faithful? Well, when he was with her, he did not stare openly at other women. He probably did notice them, he was a guy after all, but she had never caught him looking elsewhere when she was talking. She did not think he had it in him to cheat.

Did he want to get married? There her mind remained blank. A lot of people nowadays chose to remain single. It's not like he had to live like a monk if he did not marry. Maybe he was not the marrying kind and that is probably why none of his other relationships had worked out. Except for mentioning it in passing, he had never spoken about them again and she had not asked.

Then she smiled at herself ruefully. She had only discovered the depth of her feelings for him like a minute ago and she was already worried about the future, marriage etcetera. This was probably another hidden quality that love brought out in people – insecurity.

It would not take a psychiatrist to interpret her dreams that night. She dreamt that she was in a boat, a little bamboo raft, rowing through really swift waters. She was enjoying herself tremendously when all of a sudden, the skies opened up and it started raining. The torrential downpour almost obscured the horizon and she could not see anything, with rivulets of water running down her eyes and face and her clothes were soaked to the skin. It rained for what seemed like hours and the raft was moving along in the unrelenting shower. She was miserable, cold and shivering, with nobody to help her for miles. Then, out of nowhere, there was Arjun in the raft, holding a huge and sturdy looking umbrella in one hand and a steaming cup of soup in the other. He held the umbrella over their heads and handed the soup to her. She moved towards him and found life-affirming warmth in his embrace. It was as she was cosily curling into her blankets that she roused out of the dream. She could not help but chuckle, recollecting what had gone on in her subconscious. No wonder she could not resist Arjun. Even in her dreams, the man offered shelter and food. What woman in her right mind would not fall in love with him?

But did he love her? That was the million dollar question. Did he see a future with her? One part of her said he did have deep feelings for her; maybe it was not yet love but it was definitely heading there. He was protective of her, he had been hurt when she hadn't understood him and he seemed to like spending time with her.

And then the cautious part of her, the same one that drove her to carry an umbrella when the weather was slightly overcast, even though the weathercasters predicted a perfectly sunny day, reminded her that he had broken up with girls before. In the beginning, he had not even been sure if he was attracted to her.

How did one find out if one's special someone was serious about a relationship or not? Were there clues? Should she look for giveaways? Or better yet, should she outrightly ask him? Hypothetically, how would that even work? Should she declare her feelings and ask him how he felt? But what if he did not feel the same way and she was left feeling like a fool, after having said the magic words?

What if he was comfortable with just dating and did not want more? What if he was not the marrying kind and that is why he had stayed single? Could she continue to date him if she knew they were not heading anywhere? But how could she just cut him out of her life? Arrrgghh!

So many questions tumbled around in her head and there were no easy answers to any of them. It was

A Prearranged Love

too much to deal with complicated issues like love and commitment first thing in the day. Rekha resolved to not think about it anymore.

In the end, it was Sheela who unwittingly gave her the impetus to broach the topic with Arjun. On Wednesday, Sheela casually said, "It's been a while since you met Karan. How will you find a suitable guy if you don't even meet anyone?"

Rekha was completely caught off guard with the question. It had been weeks since the issue of finding 'suitable' boys had even come up, so she had completely forgotten about it. Count on Sheela to remind her; she had probably been waiting for the right moment.

Rekha was in no mood to deal with meeting some random guy at the moment. She had enough issues with just the one she was dating. Hoping to put the matter to rest, she said firmly, "I am not in the right frame of mind now, Mom. I'll let you know when I want to meet someone again."

Sheela looked at her intently and said, "You are too busy meeting friends nowadays but remember, finding someone to spend the rest of your life with is important too. Don't neglect that."

Rekha felt irritated, but Sheela was justified in saying what she did. Rekha knew how lucky she was to have an understanding mother like Sheela; the average Indian parent would not be so open-minded about their children's wishes when it came to marriage.

Sheela was not blind or oblivious; she surely had questions and concerns about Rekha's so-called 'friendship' with Arjun but she was giving Rekha her space. Guilt and cowardice assumed equal parts in Rekha's mind. She could not say anything to Sheela without first knowing where she stood with Arjun. It was not exactly fair but it was the way it was.

Over the next few days, Rekha day-dreamed about what Arjun might say when she confessed her feelings. The fervent optimist in her imagined that he would hug her, give her a long kiss and exclaim, "I love you too!" If this was a Hindi movie, she imagined this would be the moment when rousing music would play and hundreds of back-up dancers would burst into a song to celebrate their love.

The pessimist, not to be left behind, cautioned her that life was hardly as picture-perfect as in a romantic movie or book, and at worst Arjun would get freaked out like he had when they had first met and say, "I don't love you. You scare me, Rekha. I don't ever want to see you again." At best, he would be confused and slightly less freaked out and say, "I don't know how I feel and I need more time." Then he would leave and never call her again.

Saturday arrived soon enough. Rekha had deliberately suggested a restaurant for lunch this time because she did not want to be distracted by a movie or some other activity. She knew she would not be able to focus on anything except the big discussion. Her palms were damp; she felt cold and had nervous flutters in her belly. It was like she had the flu.

She had never felt this tense about anything in her life. She chose a turquoise blue top and a white and turquoise skirt because blue was a soothing colour and she desperately needed to stay calm.

She wanted to ask the 'big question' towards the end of lunch so if it got awkward, they could leave instead of sitting through awkward conversations and tense silences.

When she saw him striding towards her in the restaurant, her heart skipped a beat and then resumed its function. The setting reminded her of their first meeting and she hoped that it would not end as badly as that one had. Maybe it was the newly realised love but Arjun looked especially handsome. He was dressed in dark blue jeans and a white short-sleeved T-shirt and looked so sexy and vital that she could not help the instinctive smile that came to her lips.

"Hi!" He greeted her as he sat down across her.

"Hi" She greeted back. Stop killing him with the witty banter, Rekha, she chided herself. But she could not help it. It was one thing to decide to postpone the heavy discussion till later but suddenly she felt tongue-tied in a way that she had not been even at their first meeting.

"How is work?" She asked in a bid to recover the conversational thread.

"It's been good. We are working on some big releases so I've been quite busy. Sachin mentioned that we might have approvals for the corporate video soon."

"Oh, that's good. I have been working on the script and storyboard but it would be good to get the actual shooting started." Work for Softech was at a stage that involved a lot of back-and-forth of approvals and modifications.

Arjun launched off into a funny story about his colleagues and she started relaxing a little bit. She might as well enjoy herself while she still had a chance.

During the main course of pasta and cheese balls, there was a lull in the conversation. Rekha wondered if she should broach the subject of his previous relationships. But how does one casually interject that into a conversation, "Would you like some of my spaghetti? And by the way, how did your last relationship end?"

She remembered the conversation she had with her mother about men and their obsession with sports and said, "Last week, when you left like that, I was upset and confused. So I told my mom what happened and she said my father used to do the same thing."

"Your father also left your mom at her house after an argument?" he asked with raised eyebrows.

"Very funny. Turns out, he was also obsessed with sports, especially cricket, like a certain software guy I know."

"Hey, we are not 'obsessed' with sports. We are competitive and we play to win. It's a man thing." He shrugged as if that explained it all.

"If women said that, we would be labelled 'aggressive bitches' but you guys get away with a lot of bad behaviour."

"What bad behaviour?" he looked offended.

"Shalini told me that you almost made her cry once during a game of cards." Rekha said smugly.

"She told you that? Typical women, all gossipy even though you two had just met."

"Well, women bond faster in the company of jerks. Save the Sisterhood and all that."

"I thought you were gonna be extra nice to me today but you are even meaner, if that's possible."

"Poor baby. Maybe this will help." She picked up his hand lying on the table and kissed his palm.

"I don't know Rekha. It might take more. You did hurt the most sensitive part of me, my manhood." He said gravely.

"Hey, I was nowhere near your manhood. Your family jewels are safe from me, mister."

He sputtered out the water he had just sipped. He

laughed and shaking his head, said "Sometimes you say the most outrageous things, Rekha."

"I don't like to be predictable." If this surprised him, then she was soon going to knock him flat, Rekha thought dryly.

It was all going so well, she had set a nice stage to reveal her feelings, so Rekha still could not quite believe how quickly it all went downhill.

They were reminiscing about their trip to Mumbai and Rekha mentioned how she loved to travel, especially on work, because she got the real experience, not a tourist's carefully crafted, 'just-the-good-parts' version.

Arjun agreed and said, "I know. In fact, I have been asking my manager for on-site visits to the USA or UK where we have some clients and the prospects are looking pretty good. A couple of colleagues have already gone there and I am pretty sure I will be next."

Rekha went blank for a moment before she recovered. She was surprised at how hard the news hit her. Arjun might not be in Hyderabad a few months later. The thought left her feeling as if she was going to lose her best friend. In a way, he had become one of her closest friends in a short time. Almost all her weekends had been spent with him and now it had become a ritual. What was she going to do without him? She would never hear his infectious laugh, his wisecracks or wacky impressions.

Then she had an even more appalling thought. He had mentioned his travel as an afterthought, not as a significant piece of news to be shared with someone important. Maybe this was the answer to her unasked question. He had probably intended their relationship to be a brief experience all along.

She could not even be mad at him in all fairness. He

had not made any promises and more importantly, she had not asked for any. She had assumed they would give dating a try and had not thought beyond that. She had not expected to fall for him. She, who had mocked people who declared that they had fallen in love at first sight and other corny romanticisms, was now at the receiving end. Rekha was not in the mood to appreciate the irony as she was feeling a little surreal about the whole thing.

Dimly, she was aware, of making some remarks to Arjun in response to his casual comment but mostly, she just felt despair. In a strange way, she felt that if she had told him she loved him and he had said 'no', that would have been less hurtful. But this was much worse. Dropping this bombshell just implied that she did not figure in his future at all, she was an afterthought, a 'by-the-way...' person.

The fact that it was all due to her expectations did not matter. She felt betrayed and angry. Her soft, tender feelings towards Arjun and the resulting rosy outlook disintegrated. What was the point in confessing her feelings now? If she was not important enough to warrant more than a 'by the way...' revelation, she was not going to share the deepest feelings she had ever had for a man with him. He did not deserve it.

Instead, with significant difficulty, she summoned a humorous tone and said, "It's a good thing you won't be around in a couple of months. Mom's been pestering me to meet this other guy she found online." That was not entirely true and she was not proud of herself for saying it. But she did not want him to suspect that he had meant more to her than she clearly had to him. In a way she was salvaging her bruised pride too. Let him see how little impact his absence would have on her.

A Prearranged Love

He frowned and said, "You're kidding, right?"

"No, it's true. She is my mother, after all, and she is worried about my future."

"Well, you're not really going to date some loser you don't even know." He said impatiently.

"Well you were a 'loser I didn't even know' and I am here with you." She took great satisfaction in saying that.

"That's different. You shouldn't let your mom pressure you into doing things you don't like."

"Arjun, she is not forcing me to do anything. I can only find someone if I meet more guys."

"So, what, you're going to go on speed-dates with strange men?" he demanded.

"Don't judge me. What's your problem, anyway? It's not like this is news to you. Besides you wouldn't even be around in a few months' time."

"I don't know that. Nothing's decided. Besides, it's almost like you are already planning a replacement for me."

"Well, do you want me to sit around pining for you?" she asked sarcastically.

"If I had, I would have been sorely disappointed, wouldn't I? I should have known I was just the first in an assembly line of marriageable guys."

"Hold on just a minute. You have your future planned without room for me. But I shouldn't do the same?"

"Oh, go ahead and 'plan' your future. But there's a name for women like that, Rekha. You know what they call women who are out to hook a guy who'll take care of them for life? Man-trap."

And that's when Rekha lost it and threw her fork at him. She was so furious, her hands were shaking and she could hear her racing heart. Arjun's quick reflexes saved him, something she wasn't wholly thankful for, because she wanted to hurt him as badly as he had hurt her. He moved swiftly to the side and the flying utensil narrowly missed his face and fell behind him.

She took a couple of hundred-rupee bills out of her wallet, threw them on the table, stood up and said, "Screw you, Arjun!" She walked out, uncaring if any of the patrons in the restaurant had seen their fight.

She walked in a daze to the parking lot, started Tanya and drove off. It was a little after two in the afternoon and the traffic was not heavy, for Hyderabad anyway. It probably explained how she got home in one piece because she had hardly paid any attention to her driving. All she had been aware of was the horrible scene she had left behind.

She strode into her house, past the hall and quickly went into her room. She did not know if Sheela was at home or not. Rekha always carried a set of keys since the door locked both ways. Frankly, she could not focus on mundane details like that when her ears were still ringing and her face felt hot. She honestly could not remember the last time she was so furious at someone. Yeah, she was opinionated and impatient but annoyance and frustration were more familiar to her than this red-hot fury.

Man-trap? He may have as well called her a prostitute; it wouldn't have been any less insulting. And he had not yelled it out loud; he had said it precisely, almost tauntingly and all she had seen on his face was contempt. That really hurt. Whoever said the opposite of love was not hate but indifference was wrong. It was contempt, because nothing signified lack of respect or affection more than that.

It also hurt that what he had said was completely unfair. He knew her; he had spent, on an average, at least five hours every week with her for over two months now. She had never, ever played the helpless woman looking for a man. When they went out, they had always gone dutch and she had never assumed or expected him to 'take care' of the tabs just because he was the man.

She looked at herself in the mirror, her eyes were glassy and her face was red. He did not know her at all. Of all the things that had gone wrong today, in retrospect, it was not his casual mention of a future without her or his insult that crushed her the most. It was the fact that he did not really know her at all. How could he if he thought she was out to hook a husband so cold heartedly?

The silence in the room and her own face staring back at her drove her to move. She was so emotionally tired that she did not, could not think about it anymore. What purpose would it serve anyway? She went to the living room, turned on the TV and drowned the troubling silence in the room with some mindless sitcom's canned laughter.

Some maternal pampering and a lot of self-control gave Rekha the strength to avoid thinking about Arjun. Well, mostly.

Tuesday morning brought some fresh challenges at work. Softech had liked and approved the corporate film concept, essentially a thirty-second advertisement for 24-hour news and business channels. Rekha had to liaise with an external contact for the shooting and post production of the ad. Since ad films were not a service they offered to many clients, Flash did not do its own production work. It just made sense to outsource that aspect to freelancers instead of retaining full-time staff.

Normally, this was an aspect of her work that Rekha really enjoyed. Presenting a storyboard and script on paper was one thing, but seeing it translated as a film made it more real and it gave her a kick each time to oversee the whole process. When it was aired on TV, it felt good to say, 'Hey, I came up with that!'

Now, of course, she would have to go to Softech along with the videographer and be there to supervise the whole process and make sure that the result was what she had in mind and what the client wanted.

Rekha did not know what she would say if she did see Arjun. Yes, she would be cordial and polite. Nothing less would do with a client. But this was a more personal situation she was struggling with. Two and a half days of not thinking about what had happened on Saturday had driven Rekha crazy with the urge to talk to someone. Someone who knew Arjun and her history and had enough experience with these man-woman relationships to offer her sympathy, solidarity and preferably some colourful and nasty names for Arjun. Perhaps not exactly in that order.

It was no surprise then that she had spoken to Nitu for more than an hour on Monday. Nitu had, of course, been very supportive and called Arjun a big jackass, loser and some other colourful names. Rekha had been so relieved to share her feelings with someone who understood that she had poured it all out. She had sounded teary and emotional and so unlike herself.

But it was after her conversation with Nitu that she

had realised she had been a little unfair to Arjun. Yes, she didn't feature in his future. So what? He had not taken advantage of her in any way or misled her. And she had sort of started the argument by saying she was happy he was not going to be around so she could date other guys. That did not exactly make her look good. Of course, he was still a big jerk for calling her cruel names and breaking her heart.

Now that she had reflected on it in a calmer frame of mind, she pictured herself leaving the restaurant after throwing a fork at him, and she had an additional emotion to claim. Along with being hurt and broken-hearted, she was now embarrassed.

She had behaved so childishly and attacked the man, who was still her client. She did not think Arjun was mean-spirited enough to bring it up at work or tell his boss. But then, she had not thought he was capable of hurting her so badly either. She clearly was not a good judge of men.

The only thing that she could do was pray she would not have to deal with him again and be extra-professional in the event that she did run into him.

Chapter Nine

She was lucky the first time she visited Softech in the following week. She met with Sachin to discuss the upcoming shoot, access to the areas they would feature, the people who would be on camera and so on. Arjun's absence drove her to speculate if he was around somewhere but had declined to join them. Sachin was frequently out of the office on work and that was one of the reasons why Arjun had been her point of contact.

"Will anybody else be joining us?" She asked in a casual tone.

"No, Arjun's team is pretty busy right now with a product release. The deadline is in a week so he wasn't able to spare the time.

"Well, I am very excited; this is actually one of the most enjoyable aspects of my work and I am quite eager to get started." So Arjun was busy. She was both thankful and a little bit suspicious that he had purposely avoided her but hey, if it saved her an awkward meeting, she was all for avoidance.

Deciding to take a cue from his book, Rekha thought avoidance was a great approach. It was not like she needed to speak to him regarding work. This was turning out better than she had hoped for.

Of course, the next few days proved she had spoken too soon.

A week later, Rekha impatiently pressed the elevator button in Softech's lobby. Yes, it was working. She could see the light blinking but the LED sign above the door indicated that it was still stuck on the sixth floor. She was not in the best of moods as she had been stuck in traffic for more than thirty minutes and not only was she running late but the dust, fumes and the noise made her feel filthy and drained.

She was about to give the elevator button another jab when the sign above signalled that it was finally moving down. "Thank god." She sighed and stood tapping her foot. The elevator arrived with a loud 'ding', the doors slid apart and as Rekha entered she saw Arjun standing inside. Even though she was expecting to run into him at some point, she was frozen with a sudden realisation.

He still had the same bloody effect on her. It was naive of her, perhaps even stupid to have been so worried about her behaviour the last time. What she should have worried about was how seeing him would affect her. He looked good, dammit! She felt like she had wandered into a party where she knew no one and then suddenly spotted a good friend. For a moment, when she had first seen him, she had felt like smiling. Despite what had happened just a few days ago. It was proof that she was a dumbass.

Because standing there with her mouth hanging open like a fish was not an option, she simply said, "Hi." She suppressed her urge to smile because she was taking professionalism only so far.

He seemed surprised for a moment and said, "Hi."

This was the man who had whispered naughty things to her in a crowded and dark theatre not too long ago. Now they were making awkward elevator conversation.

She did not know if saying anything at this point would make the situation worse or better and frankly, she did not know what to say. So she walked in, stood a little ahead of him but with her back towards him so there was no need to make forced small-talk. She briefly wondered if taking her phone out and making pretend calls would be deemed as too pathetic. But the silence was excruciating and the elevator was moving too slowly.

When he called her name out her heart almost stopped. Coward that she was, she did not want to talk to him now and his serious tone indicated that he did not want to talk about the latest shenanigans on The Big Bang Theory. If they eventually did have a conversation it was going to be embarrassing and hurtful so she was not really looking forward to it.

What a time to be stuck in an elevator with no one else around! She was wondering how to answer Arjun when the elevator stopped on the next floor and two men got in. They gave her curious looks and exchanged hellos with Arjun. She offered a perfunctory smile in return and gave a small sigh of relief.

The doors slid open on her floor and seeing Arjun engaged in some techie discussion with the other two, she used her escape route and fled down the hallway to the room where she was supposed to meet Sachin. She was pretty sure she saw some curious looks thrown her way, not only because she was not a Softech employee but also because she was almost running. She was pretty sure Arjun was done with his big release and would join their meeting today. She was okay with that and had even prepared herself but she was not ready to be alone with him.

She did not have a lot of moral high ground to stand on. If she had calmly sailed out of that restaurant when he had insulted her, she could have held on to her righteous indignation and hurt and ignored him. But she had thrown a fork at him. In a restaurant. Where at least a dozen people must have seen them. She had never acted so impulsively or irrationally in her life.

Arrrgghh! She was like one of those 'Glenn Close' type jealous girlfriends who threw things and hurt people. While she had been very entertained by those movies, she had never heard of anybody acting that way in real life, especially not her!

What if somebody had filmed it on their cell phone camera and she ended up seeing it on YouTube or received an 'LOL, you've got to see this email, forward? In her era of citizen journalism and social media, she was not paranoid to imagine the possibility.

Sachin walked into the room, putting an end to her irrational musings. He had just settled in when Arjun walked in and nodded at her.

She nodded back at him and said 'Hi.' She was pretty sure her accompanying smile, if it could be called that, was weak. But it was to prevent Sachin from picking up on the not-so-cozy vibes in the room.

She quickly briefed both of them on the upcoming shoot and the things they would need for that to take place smoothly. The plan was that the CEO would speak about Softech and its vision, mission and so on, followed by the CFO who would persuade the public to invest in the company. The film crew was going to shoot a longer video that would then be edited to make a snappy 30 second advertisement. As part of the video, employees and their work would also be featured.

"We could ask for a few volunteers who are camera-friendly." Sachin suggested.

"If we ask for volunteers, we may not get the best people. I've seen it happen – enthusiastic people step up but they may not necessarily look good on camera. Why don't you two think about it and pick some staff? They need to be presentable and not be camera conscious. We need about four or five nominations. Preferably an equal split between men and women, because it looks good for the company."

Sachin looked at her bemusedly. "So you basically want me to pick looks over brains?"

Even though he had only meant it as a joke, Rekha answered it seriously. "Not necessarily. I didn't say handsome or pretty people. They need to be presentable on camera; as in even features, expressive and friendly faces. Of course, dimples never hurt." She finished with a grin.

Her gaze unwittingly went to Arjun and she saw that he was looking at her mouth. She blushed and hastily averted her gaze. That was his contribution to the meeting – not saying anything and staring at her lips?

She was not sure if Sachin had noticed how little Arjun had spoken and maybe she was taking professionalism too far but she did not want any suspicions raised.

To that end she said brightly, "Arjun, you know the guys and girls in your team well. Why don't you talk to a few of them and see if they want to be part of this?"

To top her suggestion, Sachin said, "Actually, I think you should be on camera yourself, Arjun. This guy here is quite the stud." He added proudly to Rekha.

Little did he know, thought Rekha to herself. Then she saw Arjun's less than enthusiastic reception to Sachin's suggestion and could not quite suppress the grin that spread on her face. Being on camera was not easy for most people, even if it involved a script. She had seen a few senior managers sweat through interviews and press conferences. And she could just imagine the teasing the 'stud' would get from his colleagues.

"That's a great idea. I am sure you'll have no problem saying a few lines, right?" She hoped the glee did not come through in her voice.

No such luck. He narrowed his eyes at her and said, "I guess that could work. But you'll have to coach me, you know, help me rehearse, etcetera."

Shit! "I am sure we can work out something." She said noncommittally. This is why you should not laugh at other people's misery. It would definitely come back and haunt you in some way, she chastised herself.

They discussed some other details and then Rekha implemented her speedy exit strategy. She looked at her watch, pretended to be shocked at what she saw and said, "Oops, look at the time! I have got another client meeting, so I'll just see myself out."

She purposely avoided eye-contact with Arjun, and

walked out. It could have been much worse.

Women really were the root of all troubles on earth, vowed Arjun, as he watched Rekha hurry out of the room. They were far more confusing than those 'do-it-yourself' instruction booklets. And the way she had run away from him, both earlier and now, was very insulting. It was not like he was desperate to talk to her or anything.

Well, okay, he did want to talk to her but from the way she had reacted, one would think he was a serial killer or an obscene stalker, not someone with whom she had had lunch just a few days back.

Just thinking of that lunch made him groan. She was probably still mad at him because of what he had called her. Probably? Make that definitely. She had almost taken his eye out; she obviously had some strong feelings on the subject. But he had enough provocation. When she had first mentioned dating somebody else, he had been irritated because he had assumed she was just bowing to pressure from her mother. He knew she was very close to her and would do a lot of things to make her happy.

But then she had gone on about how she wanted to get married and she could not do that if she did not meet other men. He went from being annoyed to furious and when he got angry, really angry, he did not yell or shout. He said mean things, sarcastic things with dead calmness that tended to hurt more. A lot of people in his life had borne the brunt of his wrath and while some of them had deserved it, a few others did not.

Of course, his mother would say that was no excuse to insult someone, especially women. He never had a good track record with Rekha anyway.

Damn his guilt! He was still pissed at her but seeing her today, all of his anger had been temporarily put on the back-burner and his most primal urge had been to talk to her and apologise if need be. He did not understand it himself. A couple of days ago, he had been ready to forget the whole thing and move on. That had been new for him as well. Before, he had never taken such fights so seriously. He had figured, sooner or later, his girl would call and make up with him. And they always did. But with Rekha, he had felt a burning rage and had thought, "Screw her". Then he saw her standing outside the elevator and he was desperate to talk to her.

Maybe he should call her. But what if she did not take his calls? Then he had a brainwave. He knew there was one thing Rekha put above anything else in the world – work. That's the string he would pull.

Well, that did not take long, Rekha thought to herself when her cell phone buzzed and she saw the caller's name. Given that he had worn a persistent look on his face when she had left him yesterday, she had expected him to call her. What was puzzling her was why he wanted to talk to her. Given the way things had ended between them, she did not understand his motive. And ignoring his calls would not give her any answers.

"Hello" she said crisply.

"Hi, Rekha! How are you doing?" That was casual enough. A bit too casual, she thought.

"Not too bad. What can I do for you?" There, very professional and very different from their usual 'What's up' banter.

"Just calling to fix a time for the video prep. Remember, you promised you'd coach me on it."

"Oh don't worry, it's no big deal. You'll be fine."

"I don't want to be just 'fine'. I want it to go well and not embarrass myself or the company."

When he put it that way, she did understand his concern.

"Well, ok. I can meet with you this week." She said, looking over her calendar of appointments.

"Great, how about that coffee shop at the Observatory after work, on Friday?"

The rat! That was his plan, was it? Lure her for a date under the guise of work? He probably thought she would be over their fight by now and was offering a chance to be with him again. This way he could while away his time with her before he went abroad. After all, why bother searching for a new girlfriend when he was only going to be around for a few months?

Well, she had handled men worse than him with less effort. She said, in a very accommodative voice, "Actually, I have an idea. I'll do a group session with everyone who's going to be on camera. That way, I can address all your concerns at once. And you'll see how strange it is for everyone and be a little more comfortable with the idea. Let me speak to Sachin and fix a date. I'll keep you posted."

"Umm, sure. Thanks."

She grinned and then said, "Oh, the boss is calling. Sorry, I have to go but I'll be in touch. Bye."

Ending the call, she leaned back in her chair and thought about what she had promised. She was realistic about her chances of avoiding Arjun forever. She could not keep playing this silly game of hide and seek with him but embarrassment had kept her from approaching him and apologising for her behaviour. Now though, after his call, her anger was renewed. He thought he could pick up their relationship without so much as a mention of what had happened or even an apology! She almost could not believe his nerve.

She had been prepared for hostility, contempt and some teasing from him, but this? He was acting as though nothing had happened which just pissed her off. If she had the grace to be ashamed about her behaviour and avoid him, the least he could do was show the same decency.

If he thought she was naive enough to fall for that pretence of coffee, he was not as smart as she had assumed. No more repentance or avoidance. If he so much as looked at her the wrong way, she would show him!

Thankfully, her idea of holding a group prep session appealed to Sachin too and he quickly agreed. They scheduled a meeting the following week which would be attended by the staff they had picked to be on camera and the management as well. She, for one, could not wait.

"I know some of you may already know what to do in front of the camera. That's great and thanks for being here. Here are some printouts with tips on how to carry yourself in front of the lens and how to get over your nervousness. I'll run over the points quickly but ultimately all that matters is that you be relaxed and enjoy your brief career in acting. And in case there's trouble, that's why we have very skilled editors."

Everyone chuckled and Rekha got into the groove.

She loved presenting and engaging with clients. And her experiences with other clients had given her some great anecdotes to share so soon she had the gathering nodding along and asking questions.

And that's when Arjun decided to be cheeky.

"Could we have a brief mock-interview, just so we know what to expect? You could pretend to interview one of us and we could see how it goes."

She saw a couple of nods from others and cursed him mentally. It was Friday afternoon and apparently, the group was in a mood to play hooky. She decided to indulge them and asked, "OK, who wants to volunteer?"

Of course, human nature being what it was, nobody did and some of them looked at Arjun because it was his idea. He pretended to look reluctant and then with a big defeated sigh, said "fine".

Despite his sneaky move, Rekha felt the irrepressible urge to laugh; sometime he was hilarious. Arjun made a move to get up from his side of the table and come towards her but she was having none of that.

"Oh, you can sit where you are. I can interview you from here." It was a small boardroom table so there was absolutely no need for them to get any closer. She almost laughed at his thwarted look.

"Ok, pretend that I am the camera guy, here to talk to you. Remember, you need to speak clearly, slowly but at the same time naturally. Forget that there is a camera and it's watching your every move."

"You mean, as if we were talking to each other in a coffee shop or something?" He asked deliberately.

"Or even an office environment where you are having a casual chat with your colleague." She said sweetly.

She asked him a couple of questions to get him

comfortable and then brought the focus to his work – what he did and how it impacted the world. Unsurprisingly, he did well. He was articulate and his good looks gave him the confidence to speak in a convincing fashion. She suspected that not everyone in that room would fare as well but that's why she was there; to prompt them as needed and ensure everything went well.

It was over soon and she went on to the last topic on the agenda – clothing.

"Please don't wear plain white shirts; with these white walls as background, you may look like floating heads. Wear a bright colour, preferably in a blue, purple, orange or maroon. Black makes you look too stark or stern whereas we want to project a young and innovative company. Also, collars, V necks and round necks look great."

"Oh my god! I don't have anything to wear! I need to go shopping!" Said Arjun in a high, fluttery and feminine voice amid titters from the rest of the group. Again she wanted to hug and slap him at the same time.

The meeting ended shortly after that and Rekha was relieved that Arjun did not corner her again. It was one thing to have anger fuelling your resolve to be firm with someone but when that same person made you laugh and almost forget your resolve that was dangerous. She had been practicing a lot of scathing things to tell Arjun if he tried to get her alone but she was pretty sure she would not say any of those if he confronted her right now. She just was not in the mood — she had had a good day so far and he had been funny, damn it!

This was getting ridiculous, Arjun thought to himself. Here, he had been trying every way he could think of to talk to Rekha and she was thwarting his every move. It just proved that good intentions did not always end well.

After she had finished the prep session on Friday and left, evading him again, he decided to call her landline. It was Saturday and she would be home; this way she could not ignore his calls. And if her mother answered, she would not be able to avoid his call without having to fork out an explanation. He figured it was a win-win either way.

"Hello?"

"Hi Aunty, this is Arjun. Could I speak to Rekha?"

"Hi Arjun, how are you?"

"I am fine. How are you?" He waited impatiently for the formalities to be over.

"I am good too. Rekha has gone out, for lunch I think. Have you tried her mobile?"

Lunch? Who was she meeting? He had enough sense to realise he could not pry without arousing Sheela's suspicions.

"I tried her mobile but it went unanswered. I guess she was driving or something" he lied.

"Do you want me to tell her anything?"

Arjun was briefly tempted to say that it was an urgent business matter and Rekha should call him back as soon as possible but knew Rekha would never put up with such tricks and it would only serve to make her more furious with him.

"That's fine, Aunty. I'll try her again later. Thanks. Bye."

Who was she having lunch with? Was she meeting with another 'date?' Maybe she was just out with a friend.

He tortured himself with such speculation.

And even if she was dating somebody else, what did it matter? All he had been looking for was an opportunity to talk to her and apologise. It's not like he wanted to date her again or something.

That's it, he decided. He had really tried to make amends with her but if she did not give him the chance, well, it wasn't his problem. No more chasing, calling or guilt over his treatment of her. He was just going to forget about her.

৽

Operation 'Forget Rekha' was not working very well to say the least, Arjun rued. Because, to forget someone, you probably should not spend hours with them in close confines. And yet, here he was, having been stuck with her and the camera crew for almost two hours now. It was excruciating, having to remind himself to act cool and distant but yet somehow he kept getting caught up by her gestures, her smile and yes, damn that dimpled grin!

He had responded to her 'Hello' with a brusque nod and noted her bemused response. Then Sachin had asked him to round up the other staff for the video and Rekha had tagged along to do the preliminary prep work. She had not said anything to him but had carried on a conversation with the camera guys. He had been vividly aware of her walking behind him, asking questions and at some point he had heard her laugh.

He wondered what the camera guy had said to get such a reaction. The only good thing about this experience was that his mind was so preoccupied with Rekha that he hadn't had time to think about his imminent time in front of the camera.

He was not nervous or self-conscious but did think that mouthing a bunch of rehearsed lines was kind of corny. Not to mention the ribbing he would get from his colleagues later on.

They were shooting in two parts—first the staff then the management later. He could hardly wait to get it over with.

૭

"Why don't you have some water and try to relax. Don't worry, we have the time to get it right so don't feel like you have to deliver a perfect take right away." Rekha tried to soothe the woman; poor Meenakshi had diligently rehearsed her lines but kept stuttering or forgetting her speech during the takes. This was her fifth attempt.

While Meenakshi was gratefully taking a sip and wiping her sweaty forehead, Rekha pulled the guy directing the shoot aside.

"Listen, this is clearly not working well. Why don't we just do a Q & A with her; that'll put less pressure on her and the delivery will be more natural." Rekha suggested.

"That was our original plan but then she pulled out her sheet with her lines on it; she'd clearly worked hard on it so I didn't want to discourage her."

Rekha grinned at that. "I appreciate that. A lot of people think they are auditioning or something whenever we suggest a shoot. Gives them a chance to try out 'acting.'"

He laughed and said, "Hey, I have no problems. It's your money. These people can try out all their aspirations if they want."

She laughingly wagged her fingers at him and he strode off. She turned to join the group and saw Arjun staring at her narrowly. She nodded at him but wondered what he was up to now. He had not tried to talk to her or get her alone today. She did not entirely trust his silence, especially after Sheela had told her about his call on Saturday. She had been caught off-guard when Sheela had asked if Arjun had managed to get in touch with her. Of course, she had realised that Arjun had tried to pull a fast one on her by calling her landline.

Well, she had work to do and people to soothe. Thankfully, the interview method worked better than the recital so things started rolling smoothly after that. In fact, the people involved were sportive and patient.

She was just sharing a joke with one of the guys who had finished his piece when she realised that Arjun was staring at her again. The guy she was talking to saw her looking at Arjun and he gestured to him to come and join them. Great, Arjun was blowing hot and cold today and now she had to make polite conversation with him. Joy!

"Hey Arjun, it's your turn next. We have all humiliated ourselves in front of the camera. Over to you, now."

Rekha laughed and said, "Oh, you guys weren't bad. It just takes a little getting used to, that's all."

"Yeah, you guys were doing great. In fact, I know Rekha really enjoyed your performance."

Rekha looked at Arjun. That was... weird. But then, he'd been acting weird the whole day.

Shrugging off her mental wanderings, she said, "It was certainly entertaining, for sure."

"Yeah, I wish things were more spontaneous, though. You know those viral videos where people fall off the slide or slip from the diving board or you know, throw a fork at their lunch companion, who ducks quickly? Those are just so much fun."

Rekha looked at Arjun in disbelief. Was he actually talking about their personal issues in front of strangers? He had some nerve; if she had a fork with her now, there would not be a chance to duck to safety.

Oblivious to the hidden undercurrents of their discussion, the other guy, (why could she not remember his name?), asked, "I haven't seen that fork video. Do you have it in email, if so, send it to me."

"Yes, Arjun. Send it to me too. It sounds hysterical. Of course, you know, to have a fork thrown at you, you've got to have done something really bad, huh?"

The other guy chuckled too. "Yeah man, remember Bush with that shoe thrown at him? It's the same thing."

Smiling grimly at Arjun, Rekha said, "Very true. Now, as you said before, it is Arjun's turn to act. Let's see how well he does, shall we?"

Unfortunately, it turned out that snakes could act really well. He did not even stutter or grope for words. Damn the man! But at least the shoot was halfway through. Between now and the management interviews, they were going to record some stock footage of the building, the landscaping and some people-at-work scenes. Of course, Arjun was tagging along to show the crew some good locations. She was actually looking forward to that, because the next time he so much as said the wrong thing, she was going to pounce like a ninja. He certainly had it coming.

She did not have to wait for long. They were outside, shooting the greenery around the building, when he said, "that certainly didn't take you much time." He could have been talking about the shoot but something about his inflection on 'you' alerted her.

"I don't know what you are talking about."

"I was referring to your search for the next Mr. Rekha."

"Cut the crap and say what you mean, Arjun. Unlike you, I have work to do."

"Yeah, sure. You were very friendly with that camera guy, but it's all work, right?"

"Don't be a jackass, Arjun. You sound like a psycho."

"I wasn't the one who threw a fork at someone during lunch."

"I was provoked, just like I am being now."

"Ooh, what are you gonna do, Rekha? Kick me? Hit me, bite me, maybe?"

Suddenly, all she could remember was Edward Cullen's fangs from Twilight and herself as sullen Bella; it was all too much.

She broke out in giggles first and then her laughter gained volume as she imagined Arjun sparkling in the sunlight like vampires supposedly do. Her shoulders shook and tears leaked out of the corners of her eyes. Arjun was staring at her in surprise and said, "You are the most insane woman I have ever met."

"Says you, psycho!" she snickered.

"Okayyy, what brought that on?"

She calmed down a little bit to explain. "You reminded me of Edward, that creepy, stalker vampire from the Twilight movies." He looked blank.

"Seriously? You've never heard of Twilight? You need to keep abreast of pop-culture, Arjun."

"Fine, my ignorance knows no bounds, why don't you enlighten me?"

"Well, Edward is this teenage vampire, well, not really since he is like a hundred years old. But he is a good vampire, you know. Not the bloodsucking kind. Not with Bella anyway. Bella is this girl that he falls in love with and fights with a werewolf to win her affections."

He looked dubious. "Really? Sounds kind of juvenile."

"Yeah and that's why it's fun. Edward is all pale and intense and sparkly. Bella is all pale and sulky and whiny. It's all very amusing."

"You are not one of those people who go to bad movies to make fun of them, are you?"

"Well, yeah. It's a classic case of 'it's so bad that it's good'."

"I don't get it."

"And I don't get guys who sulk because they didn't get to win a go-karting race." He glared at her.

She shrugged. "It's not a perfect world."

"True, but at least it got you talking to me again." He grinned.

"Not so fast. Our conversation only lasted this long because I got to insult you twice in the last five minutes."

"And how is that different from our normal conversations?" he mocked.

She chuckled. Then remembered that sharing jokes and laughing together was not the way to be mad at someone.

"I still stand by what I said. You are a rude, arrogant jackass."

"You attacked me with cutlery! I could have gone blind."

"Serves you right; you called me a prostitute!"

"I did not. I don't exactly remember what I said, but I know I didn't call you that."

"How convenient... You said, and I am not paraphrasing here, 'Rekha, you're a man-trap.'"

"Ok fine, but I had my reasons. You were already planning your next date while you were having lunch with your current date... and you call me 'rude?'"

"What do you expect me to do, Arjun? I am looking to get married. You know that. We met because of that. You told me that you may leave the country in a couple of months ever so casually. What did you think was going to happen after you left?"

"But it's not like I am leaving tomorrow. We can still spend time together. We enjoy spending time together anyway, so what's the harm?"

The idiot was not getting her point at all. And she could not very well say, 'because I care about you more than you obviously do for me, dumbass. It was not the right place and she was not sure there ever would be a right time for putting one's heart on display and getting it crushed.

She sighed, defeated. "There's no harm but there's also no purpose to it. That's why I don't wanna see you again, OK? Please, let's not talk about this anymore."

He must have seen something on her face because he did not pursue it.

That night, Rekha lay in bed, thinking about her conversation with Arjun. The facts were these – he was a jerk sometimes, cruel and sneaky, but he was also sweet, funny and she wanted to be with him. She did not know why she was so sure of that, could not explain it to herself, let alone anyone else. When she was with him, life just got... very interesting. She thought back to their first date, well, technically their second date, at the theatre; the movie that they had not even finished watching, through no fault of the film. She had never walked out of a movie, even a really bad potboiler.

He obviously did not feel the same way about her or he did not want to, judging from his reaction to what she had said earlier. She had been prepared for rejection and hurt when she had decided to tell him how she felt. Yet, her feelings still took her by surprise. She laughed grimly, thinking about heartbreak as it was portrayed in books and movies. She ate and slept just fine; it was afterwards that she felt dull, unexcited and empty. Work kept her focused but during those stray moments while driving or getting up in the morning and facing the inevitable day ahead she felt lost and aimless. Today was the first time in days that she had felt a rush of excitement when she had sparred with Arjun.

All that did not mean she was dumb enough to keep seeing him till he left for the US. She had her pride and she did not want to make it any harder on herself to forget him. She needed to move on with her life but just the thought of another man left her feeling sick. How did people date so casually these days, without feeling guilty or losing their head and heart?

"Then she says, 'it's fine'. You know, with emphasis on 'fine'". The two guys groaned and shook their heads in unison.

Arjun could not help listening to his colleagues' conversation. His interest had caught on when one of them had mentioned a fight with his girlfriend—after all, it was a topic close to his heart. He wanted to solve the Rubik's Cube that was the female mind. One minute you have a great rapport with a girl, you joke, you laugh and then the next minute, she says there is no point in hanging out together anymore. All because of a silly argument. How about some forgiveness, huh?

Next to him, the conversation continued. "So what did you do then?"

"What could I do? I kept nagging her till she told me what the problem was."

"Yeah, if someone nagged me like that, they would get a fist in the face. But women seem to like that we care enough to nag."

Hmm...interesting. Maybe he should continue to try and talk Rekha into dating him. Persistence, as they say, eventually pays off.

"I finally found out that she was mad because I have not told my parents about her yet. She thinks it's because I don't really love her." He made a face to indicate how ridiculous that was.

"What did you tell her?"

"Same thing I told her before. It's not the right time, man. My sister's getting married in a couple of months and I thought my parents would be in a better frame of mind after the wedding. Of course, she doesn't believe me. She thinks that maybe I am not ready for a commitment."

The guys chuckled. "Sure, it's pretty scary to consider marriage but I know she wants a commitment so I guess I'll tell my parents soon."

Arjun laughed to himself, thinking about the big 'M' word, when the epiphany struck him. Was that what Rekha wanted from him? Then he mentally smacked himself for being so dumb. Of course she wanted to get married; she had told him as much. He had just never connected the dots. He liked her, very much so, but marriage? That was just too much and too soon to think about. Maybe he was over reacting – maybe she wanted to get married but not to him. But, if so, why not? Wait, did he want her to get married to him but he did not want to get married to her?

This was confusing, he thought. It deserved some deep thought about his goals in life.

Chapter Ten

It just so happened that he did not get enough time alone with his thoughts. It all started out innocuously enough; his mother asked him to take her to the temple on Wednesday. There was some sort of special prayer happening later than usual so she had asked him to come along. While he was not big on religion, he was happy to do this for her. His mother was generally pretty independent. The only reason she had asked him to accompany her was because the auto rickshaws were on strike that day and buses were not the most reliable means of transport in the city.

So he left work early and took her to the temple. After a thankfully brief amount of time, the prayers and rituals were over and the priest distributed the *prasad* to the people milling around the deities. Arjun looked at the little cups of *Pongal* and tamarind rice with anticipation. Nothing tasted quite as delicious as the offerings from a temple pooja. He was about to shamelessly dig into the delicacy when his mother requested the priest for another cup of rice.

"Mom, I am not a pig; I won't finish the whole cup so we'll have some leftover for dad."

"Oh, it's not for him. You know Sheela lives close by so I thought it'd be nice to bring her some offerings as well. It's been a while since I met her."

"Mom, not tonight! I just feel like going straight home." Couldn't he get any peace around here?

Sunita took to cajoling him then. "I promise I won't be long. Plus, you can talk to Rekha while we are there so it's not like you'd be bored or something."

In this case, he would rather be bored to death than be around Rekha. He felt confused, uncomfortable and for some weird reason, guilty. And that annoyed him even more. He had nothing to feel bad about, he had treated her with respect, had not cheated on her or broken any promises. She had no reason to be mad at him. And if that argument sounded a bit weak even to him, well, he did not want to dwell on it.

He realised he had a more immediate situation at hand needing his attention. Left with no other choice, he agreed to take his mother to her friend's house. Sunita probably blamed his ungracious acceptance to laziness and did not suspect any other motive.

Since it was a week day and late in the evening, he did not dare to entertain hopes of Rekha not being at home. So when she opened the door to their knock, he had enough time to appear courteous and casual. She also did not reveal anything more than surprise at seeing them and welcomed them warmly. He thought that was probably due to his mother's presence.

Gesturing them to sit, she went inside to summon Sheela. Arjun used the opportunity to take in his surroundings. All bold colours and contrast, it reflected Rekha's personality. The only other time he had been here, he had been too busy to pay attention to the decor. Just keeping his and Rekha's stories straight about the movie they had supposedly watched had consumed all his thought. He smiled thinking of that evening. He had still not gotten around to watching Sherlock Holmes.

Interrupting his musings, Rekha returned with her mother and if he had not been so uncomfortable, he would have laughed at the irony of the situation. Just when he wanted to avoid someone, fate landed him right there in her living room!

Sheela greeted him and asked, "How's work, Arjun?"

"Not bad, aunty. Keeping me busy."

"He is leaving for the US in a couple of months where he'll be working on site."

"Wow, that's great. Working abroad will be a good experience for you."

He could not help looking at Rekha; seeing her guarded, curiously blank expression, his earlier suspicions were confirmed.

Sheela caught him looking at Rekha and sent an assessing look at her daughter.

She said casually, "Sunita, you came at the right time. I bought some sarees today at that new showroom on S.P road. Come and I'll show you what I got. Rekha, keep Arjun busy for a few minutes. We won't be long."

Sunita caught his mutinous look and sent him a pleading one in return. Since Sheela practically dragged his mother to her own room, there wasn't much he could do.

"Do you want some water?" Rekha asked, probably to break the vacuum in the conversation.

Unwittingly, that brought up another memory and he smilingly asked her, "Do you always offer water when you are uncomfortable?"

She smiled a little. "That depends. Are you going to smack me on the back as a thank-you?"

"Those were good times, eh?"

"You're talking as if it happened years ago; it was just a few weeks back."

Arjun did not know what made him say what he said then. "True and yet you have already planned your next date."

Instantly the smile vanished from her face. "Don't you dare talk to me like that! You're the one going away, without as much as an 'I'll miss you' and you expect me to hang around pining for you? You have some nerve."

He felt a twisted sort of satisfaction on seeing her reaction. His barbed comment had confirmed once and for all that she really had feelings for him. Now he felt guilty for bringing that up.

Softening his tone, he said, "Listen, I never meant to hurt you. I mean, I never made any promises to you or anything. I just really liked you and wanted to know if you felt the same way. And you know we had a lot of fun together."

Oddly enough that seemed to rile her even more. "You arrogant jackass! I don't care what you meant or didn't mean to do. You are the most insensitive person I've ever seen and I am glad you won't be around in a few months."

Getting a little defensive, he said, "Hey, it's not that I don't like you. I really do, but it's too soon to make any promises. We have known each other only for a few months, I am just being realistic, that's all."

"Bullshit! You're not being realistic – you're being a chicken, too scared to even consider making promises, that's all. Grow up, Arjun! You can't know anything for sure – things may change in a moment. When I first met you, I never imagined that I would run into you again let alone date you. All you can be sure of is how you feel and trust your instincts. If you don't want to commit, just say so. Don't pretend that you're being practical."

That stung. "Fine, I don't want to commit. Are you happy now?" he burst out churlishly.

She just glared at him and shaking her head, left the room.

The room fell silent, like absolute stillness after an explosion. How was it that whenever he was with Rekha, things did not go quite the way he planned for them to? He did not even want to be here, for god's sake. And what had he done? Within minutes of being left alone with her, he had gotten into an argument, felt guilty and now, was branded a coward.

He was just about ready to end the little visit, when his mother returned to the living room, eyes sparkling with the excitement of a woman who had seen some new clothes.

He studiously avoided Sheela's eyes because she seemed to see far too much and he was sure she had noticed Rekha's absence.

They quickly said their goodbyes and when his mother asked where Rekha was, he quickly fibbed, "she got a phone call."

❧

"Everything alright between you and Arjun? You didn't speak much to him." Sheela did not waste time, firing the question minutes after the mother and son had left.

"Yeah, it's fine. We had a little argument, that's all. He was being a jerk and I told him off." Saying it out aloud, she felt a little better. It may not be the whole truth, but her head was about to explode with thoughts and she was glad to vent it out a little.

Sheela just nodded and did not ask any more questions. Rekha felt numb, but she had asked for it. She had wanted to hear it from him, the unvarnished truth. Now that she knew he did not want a future with her, so there was no need to entertain any foolish hopes. She had driven him to say it but it did not make her feel any better.

The worst part was she knew if he opened his mind up a little bit, he would see how good they were together. She was fairly sure he would not have reacted so strongly at the notion of her dating somebody else if he did not feel a little possessive about her. And he had been persistently after her to continue their relationship until now. She did not know when exactly it had sunk into his obtuse brain that she wanted more from him; then he had gotten scared of the big 'C' word.

Then she chastised herself for doing exactly what she swore she would not do. Hope. There was nothing she could do anymore – he did not want what she wanted and she was practical enough to know that decisions of the heart needed to be made wholeheartedly.

✍

A Prearranged Love

Day one after their confrontation went by uneventfully for Arjun. He went to work, had a productive day, in fact more than normally productive. He ate lunch, had casual conversations with his colleagues. All boringly, reassuringly normal. He did not miss Rekha. Clearly, he was ready to move on. It was a good thing they had had an honest talk yesterday. Yup, all was fine.

Day two was also more of the same, except for one slight change. While the casual conversations were going on, his mind sort of wandered to unwanted places. More specifically, he wondered how Rekha was doing. She must be finishing up her day right about now. She had told him that at the end of every week, she had to give a status report to her clients on the work she was doing. Even though she hated paperwork, she made a habit to do it daily so it did not pile up on Friday. Then he realised that he had missed the punch line of his colleague's joke because he was caught up in Rekha's filing habits and that got him a little annoyed.

Day three was a bit of trial but nothing he could not cope with. Somebody in his team had scheduled a meeting at eight in the morning; normally not a problem, but he had overslept that morning because he had trouble falling asleep the night before. So he was late getting to work and walked in when everybody was already seated and the presentation had started. He ignored the raised eyebrows his boss gave him but he was embarrassed and furious with himself. He tried to get up to speed and had almost succeeded when the session broke up for a small recess. He got himself a cup of coffee and still preoccupied with the presentation, he brought up his filled-to-the brim coffee cup too fast and the brown liquid splattered on his sleeve and his all new suede shoes.

"Shit!" He swore loudly and expelled a few more invectives. To add insult to injury, one of his colleagues walked up to him and said dryly, "It's not your day today, is it?"

They reconvened shortly after that so he could not even clean up the mess on his clothes. He had to sit with the warm sleeve sticking to his arm and the smell – oh god, the smell! Nothing smelled as good as fresh coffee and as bad as its stale remnants.

After that nightmare of a meeting ended a little after noon, he went back to his desk only to be swamped by emails from that morning. There was a lot of work to be done but somehow he just could not apply himself to it. He was too distracted and frankly, a little frazzled.

The final straw was the next morning. He reached office, on time but still cranky because he had had yet another night of fitful sleep. He was determined to tackle work and whatever else the day held in store for him. He had just logged in to his PC when it suddenly froze; he moved his mouse but the hourglass on the screen was alarmingly still. Just when he thought it could not get any worse, he was faced with the 'blue screen of death'.

He smacked his fist on the desk, grabbed his coffee mug and marched to the restroom. There, he flung it against the gleaming granite counters and watched it shatter into shards. He walked out of the room, let his colleague know that he was taking the rest of the day off and drove his bike till he came to a familiar place. He sat on the first bench he saw, stretched his legs and leaning back, exhaled deeply. He had never felt so frustrated in his life, so powerless against fate. Looking at the green expanse of trees and hedges, he relaxed for what was probably the first time in days. The instinct that had been nagging at him for the past few days was stronger now.

He did not want to end things with Rekha.

It was not a great epiphany, just an insistent feeling. She was right. He was scared of commitment. It wasn't backed by anything deep or psychological; it was just that feeling of 'Oh, shit, I enjoy my life now, why get married?' Well, he had certainly not enjoyed these past few days. Maybe he was ready to take that big step — marriage. He gulped just thinking about it. Baby steps. Take it slow and easy. But first, he had to tell Rekha how he felt. He hoped that she could look past her hurt and disappointment and forgive him. Would she trust him now if he told her that he was serious about her? He did not exactly have a good track record of knowing his own mind.

It would not be enough to just tell her how he felt, he had to show her – yeah, that's what he would do — a big gesture. What kind of gesture would convince her that he wanted to be with her? Instantly he thought of the corny and cheesy gestures made in Bollywood movies — pink balloons, red roses, her name spelled in the air with a jet plane or an orchestra playing her favourite song and promptly dismissed them. No, this required something more subtle. He needed to talk to somebody and get some advice. Preferably some female. Ironically this is where Rekha would have come in handy.

He thought of Shalini – she and Rekha had been pretty tight the one time they had met and she was someone he considered to be smart and sensible. Why not ask her for some suggestions? He did not have to reveal too much, and he could just refer to Rekha as his girlfriend. That would help to avoid any questions and the inevitable gibes. See, he had a plan. There was no need to panic.

He called Shalini and since their offices were nearby, his suggestion to 'catch-up' over coffee was met without suspicion. They had just sat down with their cups when, without preamble, he said, "So, there's a reason that I asked to meet today."

"I knew it! I was wondering about the sudden invitation. What's up? Do you need money or something?"

"No. It's not anything like that. This is a bit more ... tricky."

"Arjun, what did you do?" Shalini looked alarmed.

"Nothing illegal. Don't panic. I just needed some advice."

"About what? Enough with the suspense. Tell me now!"

Despite the situation, he smiled. "Nothing so dangerous as a curious woman."

She threateningly raised her fist at him which reminded him of Rekha and that made him grin goofily. Focus, Arjun, he told himself.

"Okay, it's about a girl. I am serious about her. How do I tell her that?"

She smiled like a Cheshire cat. "You've met your match, finally! I was sure you were gonna be ever-dating, never-married."

"Relax, nobody's getting married. I am just considering it, may be..." he said defensively.

"Coming from you, that's almost a wedding invitation." She mocked. "Whatever your feelings are, why don't you just tell her you are serious about her?"

"Well, there's a slight problem. I may have told her, not too long back, that I wasn't serious about her."

"Oh, so you broke her heart and now you want her back."

"Hey, I didn't break her heart, I just wasn't ready then. And now I miss her and when I think of not being with her, it just doesn't feel right."

"Aw, look at you spouting poetry. I should have recorded what you said just now and played it to your old girlfriends. And our gang."

At his look, she relented and said, "Alright, I am sorry. That was very sweet, what you just said. Why don't you just tell her that?"

"That won't work. She won't believe me and I wouldn't blame her. I've been so wishy-washy with her from the beginning that no matter what I say now, it probably wouldn't convince her. I need to show her how I feel. Maybe with a grand gesture, to make up for what I said before."

"Hmm, I see your point. How about this – something big to signify a commitment? Why don't you give her a ring?" When he looked blank, she clarified, "Not the ones with the phone; the kind you wear on your finger."

"I don't know. It seems so clichéd. What if it isn't enough? Men give women jewellery all the time. Heck, I gave my old girlfriends some stuff. I want this to be special."

"How about a special message on one of those TV channels? The ones where they play songs dedicated by callers to someone special?

"You mean those losers who send badly spelt messages followed by really silly songs? No way. Even if I wanted to, it wouldn't be feasible – she would have to be there watching the channel at that precise moment and she may not even realise it's for her from me. I need something a little more direct, Shalini."

"You are hard to please but I am glad she matters so much. Forget the big gesture part – just focus on how you feel. If she won't believe you, how about appealing through someone else? Someone close to her, someone who she trusts and listens to? Personally, if I meet a guy who I really like, I am going to want to know how my friends or family feel about him so if they vouched for him, that would be a solid point in his favour."

He seemed to consider it. "That's not a bad idea. Close friend or family... I have got it! Her mother! Re-, I mean she is very close to her mother and that's who I should talk to. Thanks, Shalini." He wondered if she had caught on to his slip-of-tongue but she seemed to be more focused on what he had just said.

"Are you serious? You're gonna tell your girlfriend's mother about your feelings? Isn't that a bit risky?"

"No." Arjun said with conviction. "In fact, I like the sound of it. Her mom is quite cool and with-the-times, you know. And this would convince her that I am serious about her."

"Okay, since you seem sure about this just let me know how it goes." As they got up to leave, she said casually, "Oh, tell Rekha I said hi."

He stopped dead and pretended not to understand. "Oh, I am not gonna see her anytime soon."

"Oh please, save it. You are gonna have to be a lot smoother than that if you're gonna talk to Rekha's mother."

Sheepishly, he said, "Sorry. How did you guess?"

She shrugged dismissively. "You insult me Arjun. I could smell that 'girlfriend' cover-up miles away."

∼

Arjun had it all planned out. He would call and ask to meet Rekha's mother. Then he would tell her that he was serious about Rekha and wanted to let Sheela know, the proper and old-fashioned way. She would be very impressed and probably appreciate his honesty. He would request that Sheela not say anything about their meeting to Rekha; that way he could meet Rekha and tell her that he was serious about her and if she refused to believe him and asked for proof, he would say, "Ask your mom. She's the proof!"

She would probably be grateful to him because he would have saved her the trouble of confessing to her mother. How do you tell your parents that you have found someone for yourself? It had to be an awkward conversation. With his help, she would not have to go through that.

Sheela would be happy. Rekha would be happy and he... he would be thinking of ways that Rekha could show her appreciation. Arjun was feeling pretty good about himself. He had taken Shalini's suggestion and really run with it. He was the man!

"How are you, Aunty?" Arjun started with the pleasantries. After all, he was talking to his, umm, prospective mother-in-law. Whoa, he'd grown-up fast, from no-commitment to saying the second most-dreaded term in the English language starting with 'M'.

"I am good. How are you?"

"I am good too. Well, actually, I am a bit confused and I don't know how to say this..." He took a deep breath, leaned forward and plunged headlong into his speech.

"I like Rekha a lot and I wanted you to know... that I am serious about her... I love her!" Whew, that had sounded a lot smoother in his head.

Sheela did not seem to notice his clumsy delivery. If anything, she had a big grin on her face. "I was hoping this would happen. I am so happy!"

Her reaction soothed his nerves a little and he gained some confidence. "I am glad you feel that way. I know how much Rekha values your opinion and I wanted to make sure you're happy with this." He congratulated himself for that bit. He was just too good.

"That's so thoughtful of you. Tell Sunita she's done an excellent job of raising you. So do you want to tell Rekha or should I?" Sheela asked with a smile.

Before he could answer, he heard a voice that did not exactly sound pleased.

"What are you doing here?" Rekha asked.

Arjun cursed silently. He had taken a half-day off from work precisely so he could speak to Rekha's mother alone. What was Rekha doing, back so early?

Sheela asked the question he had voiced mentally. "Rekha, how come you are back so early?"

"I had a headache and just couldn't concentrate any longer, so I took leave for the rest of the day."

Talk about ill-fated coincidences, Arjun mused. He had been doing so well and now he was sort of lost, wondering what he should do next. Damn, he needed some privacy either with Rekha or her mother to finish their conversation.

"I'll get some coffee for you both. Rekha, why don't you go freshen up and chat with Arjun while I do that."

Rekha glared at him, as Sheela walked away and he was left sitting there alone.

Soon, Rekha came back and sat down.

"What are you doing here?" she said in low tones.

"I came to tell you that I was wrong before. I was scared and I am sorry I hurt your feelings. I am serious about us and I just wanted to tell you that."

"You came to tell me but you chose the middle of the day when I would be away?" she asked sceptically.

"No, I knew you wouldn't be at home. See, I came to talk to your mom about us."

"What?" she shrieked. "What the hell did you want to talk to her for?"

"Well, I thought it would be better to tell her about us."

"Let me get this straight. You break my heart, then before you talk to me and set things right, you tell my mother about us??"

"What is going on here? Did you know Arjun was interested in you before? Have you been seeing each other all along?" Sheela demanded, having left the kitchen when she heard Rekha's raised voice.

He really could use the coffee now because he felt a headache coming on. Things had gone horribly, almost hilariously wrong. Almost, because he was in no mood to laugh.

"This is why I wanted her to hear it from me first, you idiot." Rekha hissed at him.

"I am so sorry, Rekha, I just wanted to prove to you that I was serious about you this time. I thought you wouldn't believe me without some sort of a gesture."

"That's why they invented Hallmark cards for every occasion, Arjun." Rekha retorted, calmer now.

"One of you better tell me what's going on. At this point, I think I almost trust you more than Rekha,

Arjun." Sheela declared, glaring at Rekha.

Rekha, in turn, glared at Arjun.

"Ok, let me explain. Aunty, I am sorry if I wasn't clear before. Rekha and I are interested in each other and we sort of went out a couple of times. But we weren't sure about a future together so we kind of broke up."

"You weren't sure, you mean." Rekha reminded him.

"Yes, I admit, I wasn't ready to commit before. But these past few days have been so bad, Rekha, and I missed you terribly. That's why I am here."

"Why didn't you both just let me and your mother know in the beginning that you liked each other?" Sheela was still trying to understand.

"Because we didn't, mom." Rekha broke in. "Everything I told you after we first met was true. I didn't think much of him. You know that. But then we met again at work and ended up spending time together. We saw sides of each other that we liked."

"So why didn't you tell me then? Why the continued pretence of friendship?"

"Well, everything was happening so fast. I was just discovering these feelings for him and I knew if I told you, you would want me to give you some sort of commitment. I just wasn't ready." Rekha finished apologetically.

Sheela frowned. "The way you two go on about commitment, one would think you were considering buying a house or property."

"Don't you think marriage is even bigger than those things? Of course we need time." Rekha said defensively.

"Marriage doesn't need time, it just needs the instinct. If your gut says he or she is the right person for you, go with your gut feeling then the rest will fall in line. Time won't change any of that."

"We don't think like your generation. We need time to prepare, mom."

"No, you prepare for death. Marriage, you just enjoy. Your generation doesn't know how to be spontaneous."

Arjun wasn't ready for an 'us versus them' generation battle. Things were still hanging in the air.

"Rekha, your mom is right. We do take time to decide. So what's your decision going to be? I've made my intentions clear. It's your turn."

She smiled sweetly. "You made your intentions clear to my mom. I still have no clue so I can't say anything till I hear the magic words."

"I said I was sorry. I really am."

"Not those, Arjun." She said enigmatically.

"What do you mean... oh no, you don't, not here??" he beseeched.

"Yup, you wanted to bring my mom into this, so man-up and say it!" She had a big grin on her face.

"You're not getting away with this, you know." Arjun said threateningly, a little later when they were alone.

"I thought I already did! I made you say 'I love you' to me in front of my mother." She laughed.

He shuddered at the memory. Revealing such personal feelings with an audience was bad enough, but when that audience was your girl's mother, the embarrassment reached excruciating proportions.

"Don't I at least get something for my courage, a reward maybe?" he ventured.

"Alright, fair enough. I did put you through a lot."

She came close, pulled him down and hooked her hands around his neck. She smilingly raised her lips, brushed them against his softly. He was sinking into the sensations when suddenly she yelled, "Mom!"

He jumped apart and whirled around to see ... nobody.

"Yup, just got away with it again." Rekha said grinning.

Acknowledgements

A million thanks to –

- My best friend Ambika who put the 'writing bug' in my head

- My dear friend and honest critic Urvashi who was the first to give me feedback

- My friend, mentor and champion Samba for his support in getting this published

- My friends Seshank, Priya and Bettina for their feedback and encouragement

- My agent Kanishka for his enthusiasm and professionalism

- My husband Sairam for his unquestioning support and laptop-sharing!

- Last but not the least, my parents, for enabling me to be everything I am today.

www.ingramcontent.com/pod-product-compliance
Lightning Source LLC
Chambersburg PA
CBHW071209260626
47162CB00004B/1231